The New
BLACK MASK
QUARTERLY

The New BLACK MASK QUARTERLY

Number 2

EDITED BY

MATTHEW J. BRUCCOLI & RICHARD LAYMAN

A HARVEST/HBJ BOOK

HARCOURT BRACE JOVANOVICH, PUBLISHERS

SAN DIEGO   NEW YORK   LONDON

Editorial correspondence should be directed to the editors at Bruccoli Clark Publishers, Inc., 2006 Sumter Street, Columbia, SC 29201.

ISSN 0883–4512
ISBN 0–15–665480–6

Designed by G.B.D. Smith
Printed in the United States of America
First Harvest/HBJ edition 1985
A B C D E F G H I J

HBJ

Table of Contents

v

The New
BLACK MASK
QUARTERLY

Elmore Leonard:
An Interview

It has been commonplace to read confessional reviews of Elmore Leonard's novels in which a prominent critic admits he is late to sing Leonard's praises. Glitz has ended that. If it is not the most successful mystery novel of 1985, it is certainly among the most celebrated.

Glitz is Leonard's twenty-fourth novel. He began his literary career in 1953 writing westerns in the mornings before he reported to work as an advertising copywriter. Eight years and five novels later, he published Hombre, *which has since been designated one of the twenty-five best westerns of all time by the Western Writers of America. When the 1967 movie of* Hombre *(starring Paul Newman) freed Leonard to write fiction full-time, he found that the market for westerns had dried up, so he turned to mysteries, which many readers feel is the genre in which he excels. His reputation as a skilled storyteller and a master at characterization has been building with each successive novel. Herbert Mitgang has observed that the lives of Leonard's characters "add up to social commentary."*

Mr. Leonard lives in Birmingham, Michigan. He is presently working on a pilot film for an ABC television detective series to be called Wilder.

NBMQ: How do you account for the instant success of *Glitz*? Did you do something different this time?

Leonard: No, I didn't. It's an accumulation. I think it's something that's been building gradually over the years, certainly since 1980, from the time I went to Arbor House and Don Fine really got behind me. I had reached a point where I was no longer simply grateful that a publisher had accepted my work. Now I expected the publisher to do something. If they really liked my work, they should sell it. So I went from Delacorte to Bantam, and then Don Fine at Arbor House said, "I'll sell you." He proceeded to get my material into the hands of, I think, reviewers who were more prestigious as far as having an effect on other reviewers. The next four years or so reviewers began to notice me and ask, "Where have I been?" The "I" in some cases referring to the reviewer himself, though most often it referred to me. As if I had been hiding out somewhere. It was Don Fine who started this. From then on it was a matter of momentum. As more and more people began to read me, and as more reviewers began to review me all over the country, I got still more readers and my books began to sell at an astonishing rate.

I think the timing of the publication of *Glitz* was perfect: the fact that it came out when it did, right after the first of the year. Right after that Christmas rush of important titles, important authors. It came along during a sort of lull; that enabled me to get on the best-seller list to begin with. Then I got good reviews again—a good review by Stephen King, for example, in the *New York Times*. A write-up in George Will's column must have surprised everybody; I've gotten an awful lot of response from it. I don't think that the book is that much better. I've been more aware lately of trying to make each book better, but in very minor ways. It's not noticeably better written. I think you'll see the same style, the same tone, the same sound ever since '74, ever since 52 *Pick-up*, that I would call the beginning of what I'm doing now. While I have been improving in some ways, it was mostly a matter of timing. My efforts paid off. I'm going to continue to try to improve as far as that goes. I think we can always do that. But it's more in very small ways. In *Glitz*, for example, it was in experimenting with different points of view in writing the same scene. I would write it from one character's point of view and then switch around and do the scene again from another character's point of view and find that it had a lot more life in it, that it was a little more dramatic, more colorful, more interesting. I'm going to continue to do that.

NBMQ: I notice an increasing concern with sociology in your recent books. Is that deliberate?

Leonard: Well, I'm not sure I know what you mean.

NBMQ: The social structure of a city, a class of people.

Leonard: I have made more of an effort in that line ever since, I think it was 1977 or '78, when a reviewer said, "He set a story in Detroit, and he didn't take full advantage of the background of that particular city. He didn't bring it to life." I think that particular review was by an Associated Press writer, and unfortunately this review was the one that ran across the country and appeared in at least a hundred different newspapers. But I think I have learned things from reviews, ways to improve my writing.

NBMQ: You really take reviews seriously?

Leonard: Well, some. When I see that it can be helpful—because I do concentrate on backgrounds a little bit more. I certainly made more of Detroit in subsequent books. I've been more aware of it, for example, in Florida, in south Florida, in south Miami Beach when I did *LaBrava*, in Atlantic City when I did *Glitz*. It is important. It is a part of the feeling that I get when I visit there that I want to put into the book. I'll tell you something else, too. As far as sociology is concerned, I try to keep current, in that what I'm reading in the newspapers while I'm writing the book, some of it is going to get into the book. Because it's what's going on. What the characters read, there might be a reference to something—certainly what they're watching on television, a game show on television, for example. Which is part of our lives—watching television, reading the paper.

NBMQ: How do you go about researching background? Do you just osmose it, or do you go to libraries, read back issues of magazines or newspapers?

Leonard: Lately I've used a researcher, a fellow who works for a film company in Detroit. He does a lot of research for them. He's sort of on a part-time basis with them, so he has time to do work for me. He went to Atlantic City, for example. First of all, I said I want to set a story in the Atlantic City–Philadelphia area. Let's find out what's going on there. He called the New

Jersey Film Commission. They sent him some pictures, some literature on Atlantic City. He got the 1983 Pennsylvania Crime Commission report. When I decided, yeah, this is the place I want to set a story, he went to Atlantic City, came back with a file of newspaper clippings that covered the everyday activities of the city. He had it broken down into racketeering, prostitution, the unions, stories about the casinos themselves, new construction. This file is probably eight inches thick, stuffed with newspaper clippings. Then he took 180 pictures on Absecon Island from Atlantic City all the way down to Longport and then put all the pictures in order. So even before I went, I could see likely places to use as locations.

NBMQ: How much time did you spend in Atlantic City?

Leonard: I spent from Sunday through Thursday, five days. I spent one day with the Atlantic County major-crime squad, and I went over their procedures with them—how they would investigate a death, what might appear to be a suicide. For example, I said to the detective, "You've got a woman that's found on the sidewalk. She obviously fell to her death. What's the first thing you do?" He said, "I'd look up. See if there's an open window somewhere." Then he explained how he would canvass the neighborhood or the apartment building first and talk to everybody. The procedures are the same most places except that they use different forms. They may go about it a little bit differently. Then I asked the police how they would react to a cop from another jurisdiction, a cop from Miami Beach coming in there and sticking his nose into it, asking them questions and offering to help. I got their reaction to that. I said, "Assuming, of course, that you feel that there is a rapport between you and the Miami Beach cop, you get along okay, would you allow him to help a little bit?" "Sure, yeah. But I don't think I'd want my chief to know about it." Things like that. I spent time with the cops. I was introduced to the president of one of the casinos; then he handed me over to a woman who was in charge of surveillance. She took me into the monitoring room where they look at the monitors of every foot of the casino floor. Then she took me to the eye-in-the-sky where you're standing right over the tables, where you look directly down on the play. So I got a pretty good view of what goes on behind the scenes. Most of the information, of course, came out of newspaper and magazine articles. Specific stories about a guy who comes to town with a million bucks and how he's treated and what he does with it. Same thing in south Florida, in Miami Beach, I roamed around there with a friend of mine who's a private investigator, a fellow I went to college with, University of Detroit, more than thirty years ago. Roamed around there, spent some time with the Miami Beach police, one detective in particular for *LaBrava*. Asked a lot of questions about situations that appear in the book. What happens if a woman who lives in one of the hotels receives an extortion note, what do you do? What's the procedure in investigating this kind of a case? Do you bring in the

FBI? And so on. I find out exactly how they would handle the investigation.

NBMQ: You wrote westerns before you turned to contemporary crime novels. Do the two genres have anything in common? And why did you switch?

Leonard: I started out with westerns because in 1951 I had written a couple of short stories in college and they really had no purpose. There was certainly no market for them. I decided, if you're going to write, let's study a particular genre, concentrate, research and learn how to write within the framework of this genre. I picked westerns because I like western movies so much. I felt that there was a good possibility to sell them, to sell to Hollywood. I hadn't read many westerns. I began to notice the westerns in the *Saturday Evening Post* and *Argosy*. I liked the fact that in this market you could aim at magazines that were paying $850 or $1,000 for a short story and work your way down through *Argosy*, which was paying $500 to $1,000, to *Bluebook*, and then down to all the pulp magazines. There were at least a half-dozen very good western pulp magazines. *Dime Western* being, I think, the foremost one. *Zane Grey Western Magazine, Fifteen Western Tales, Ten-Story Western*, those good ones paying two cents a word, which is a hundred bucks for a short story. And that wasn't bad in the early fifties. I concentrated on the western, did a lot of research, subscribed to *Arizona Highways* for my descriptions for the settings. Did a lot of research on the Apaches and the cavalry, which was very big then.

Cowboys—what they wore, what they ate. Guns. I started reading gun catalogs. I put all that together into western stories.

I stopped writing westerns after *Hombre*. I wrote it in 1959, and it took almost two years to sell because the market was drying up. That's because of all the westerns on television. It finally came out in 1961, and I didn't write another western until the early seventies. The last one was in 1979 for Bantam because Mark Jaffe, who was the editorial director at Bantam then, likes westerns. I don't know if there is a similarity other than the western kind of a hero, that stand-up kind of a guy who manifests his attitude in *Destry Rides Again*. That's kind of the idea. Maybe it can be seen to some extent in what I'm writing now, in crime fiction. In the back of my mind I kind of think that I do sort of a *Destry Rides Again* in that my guy is, usually, misjudged. He's fairly passive. He's not a typical hero. I try to make him a very ordinary kind of individual, very realistic. A real person who finds himself in a life-or-death situation. What does he do? He's a stand-up kind of a guy, like the western hero. And by the time the antagonists realize that they've misjudged this guy, he has the situation turned around and he's coming at them. I get so caught up and interested in some of my minor characters, especially my antagonist, that every once in a while I have to remind myself that I have a hero. That even though this story is not a traditional type of crime story, still there is a hero, and he's going to have to solve the problem, whatever it is. So I have to get him to do something. Every once in a while I forget about it, that he's there. He's just sort of walking through the story and observing.

NBMQ: Many people have said the detective story or the crime story is the last refuge for the traditional, self-reliant American hero. I think this applies to your work.

Leonard: I think it does, too. Sure. I think that my work has come out of a tradition. But I don't think there's that much resemblance to the tradition that it came out of, aside from the fact that, yes, I am aware that my lead is the hero and he is going to win. There's no question in my mind the guy *is* going to win. But he's going to have my attitude in the way he does it. He's not going to be the typical hero; though when you get right down to it, he's going to be as gutsy as he has to be. My cops, I feel, are real cops. in *Glitz*, for example, when Vincent confronts Ricky, at Ricky's car, and Ricky says, "What do you think you're doing?" he takes him by the hair and the jacket, bangs him against the car, and says, "Anything I want, Rick." This is a cop talking. I try to make them as real as possible. My cops cut corners a little bit, just as the real ones do.

NBMQ: Do you regard any one of your novels as your breakthrough book? The one in which you found your approach to your material or the one in which you found your authorial voice?

Leonard: Yeah, I think looking back it would be 52 *Pick-up*. At the time I didn't realize it, but now I see that was the beginning of the voice that I've developed. Then I got into books like *Swag* and *The Switch*, where now the main characters are not the usual heroes. They're on the other side. Then I realized how much fun I could have with those people, that I don't have to make them entirely despicable. I can have fun with guys who are into crime, into the life.

NBMQ: Are you concerned with making a statement about the nature of criminal behavior?

Leonard: No, I'm not concerned with any kind of a statement. I just tell a story. My purpose is to entertain and tell a story. I'm not grinding any kind of an ax at all. My attitude comes through—*maybe* my attitude comes through. But they're not big issues by any means.

NBMQ: Are there any recurring themes that run through your fiction?

Leonard: There might be, but I'm never aware of it. I don't begin with a theme. If someone were to ask me what is the theme of *Glitz*, I'd have to stop and think, or re-read it to determine if I'm unconsciously doing anything beyond telling a story. Is there a theme? I don't know. The *New York Times* headline for the review of *Unknown Man #89* was "Decent Men in Trouble." That's probably as close as I would venture to describing my approach. Ordinary people who get into some kind of a scrape. How do they get out of it? I never know. I never have any idea how my book is going to end. I even think of Stick, in *Swag*, as a decent guy, even though he's into that life. In *Switch* I certainly didn't know how it was going to end. I knew in *Swag* that they were going to be arrested, that they were going to fail, but I wasn't sure how. In *Switch* it was kind of a tricky ending. I come up with tricky endings here and there, but I never see them coming until I get there. In *LaBrava*, when I was about thirty pages from the end, I said to my wife, Joan, "Okay, here are the three ways this book can end. These are the three things that could happen to Jean Shaw. She could be arrested; she could die; she could get away with it." It had to be one of those. My wife said, "What if . . ." and gave me a fourth option. I thought, Oh, my God. That's perfect. And it was the one I used.

NBMQ: You've said that you write to be read. You write to entertain. Do you have any image of your reader, the person you are writing for while you are writing?

Leonard: No, I don't. Because I don't picture a particular reader. I think by now I have nearly as many women as men who read my work. At least more than half the letters are from women, though I do think my books appeal more to men. When I'm interviewed one day by George Will and by Pete Hamill the next— who would appear to be poles apart in their attitudes, and yet both enjoy my work—I think: This is wonderful that I can appeal to a wide range of readers. Ideally the author wants to sell books, expand his readership, without getting caught up in the actual business of selling them. I'm happy to see *Glitz* on best-seller lists, but I hope to God I never take it too seriously. The whole idea of how I work is to be very relaxed in telling the story, to do it my own way. I certainly can't aim this book at a list—picking details that would make it more popular, appeal to more people. That's the worst thing I could do. I've got to tell my own story in my own relaxed way, with the primary purpose of pleasing myself, then hope that there are other people who enjoy it too. And that does seem to be happening now. But if I had no more readers than before, I'd still write. It's what I do.

LaBrava

ELMORE LEONARD

Reviewing LaBrava, *Alan Cheuse wrote: "the sleazy, decadent beach-front facades, mental health stations, go-go clubs and water-soaked immoralities of contemporary south Miami Beach, where antique widows cross paths with young hustlers fresh out of Cuban prisons. . . . Elmore Leonard has the feel of it; he makes us feel it—and the characters, whom we know as much by their dialogue as their actions. . . ."*

In the second chapter from LaBrava *that follows, Leonard demonstrates this basic element of his talent.*

"I'M GOING TO TELL YOU a secret I never told anybody around here," Maurice said, his glasses, his clean tan scalp shining beneath the streetlight. "I don't just manage the hotel I own it. I bought it, paid cash for it in 1951. Right after Kefauver."

Joe LaBrava said, "I thought a woman in Boca owned it. Isn't that what you tell everybody?"

"Actually the lady in Boca owns a piece of it. Fifty-eight she was looking for an investment." Maurice Zola paused. "Fifty-eight or it might've been '59. I remember they were making a movie down here at the time. Frank Sinatra."

They had come out of the hotel, the porch lined with empty metal chairs, walked through the lines of slow-moving traffic to the beach side of the street where Maurice's car was parked. LaBrava was patient with the old man, but waiting, holding the car door open, he hoped this wasn't going to be a long story. They could be walking along the street, the old man always stopped when he wanted to tell something important. He'd stop in the doorway of Wolfie's on Collins Avenue and people behind them would have to wait and hear about bustout joints where you could get rolled in the old days, or how you could tell a bookie when everybody on the beach was wearing resort outfits. "You know how?" The people behind them would be waiting and somebody would say, "How?" Maurice would say, "Everybody wore their sport shirts open usually except bookies. A bookie always had the top button buttoned. It was like a trademark." He would repeat it a few more times waiting for a table. "Yeah, they always had that top button buttoned, the bookies.

"Edward G. Robinson was in the picture they were making. Very dapper guy." Maurice pinched the knot of his tie, brought his hand down in a smoothing gesture over his pale blue, tropical sports jacket. "You'd see 'em at the Cardozo, the whole crew, all these Hollywood people, and at the dog track used to be down by

14

the pier, right on First Street. No, it was between Biscayne and Harley."

"I know . . . You gonna get in the car?"

"See, I tell the old ladies I only manage the place so they don't bug me. They got nothing to do, sit out front but complain. Use to be the colored guys, now it's the Cubans, the Haitians, making noise on the street, grabbing their purses. *Graubers,* they call 'em, *momzers, loomps.* 'Run the *loomps* off, Morris. Keep them away from here, and the *nabkas.*' That's the hookers. I'm starting to sound like 'em, these *almoonas* with the dyed hair. I call 'em my bluebirds, they love it."

"Let me ask you," LaBrava said, leaving himself open but curious about something. "The woman we're going to see, she's your partner?"

"The lady we're gonna rescue, who I think's got a problem," Maurice said, looking up at the hotel, one hand on the car that was an old-model Mercedes with vertical twin headlights, the car once cream-colored but now without lustre. "That's why I mention it. She starts talking about the hotel you'll know what she's talking about. I owned the one next door, too, but I sold it in '68. Somebody should've tied me to a toilet, wait for the real estate boom."

"What, the Andrea? You owned that, too?"

"It used to be the Esther, I changed the name of both of 'em. Come here." Maurice took LaBrava by the arm, away from the car. "The streetlight, you can't see it good. All right, see the two names up there? Read 'em so they go together. What's it say?"

There were lighted windows along the block of three- and four-story hotels, pale stucco in faded pastels, streamlined moderne facing the Atlantic from a time past: each hotel expressing its own tropical deco image in speed lines, wraparound corners, accents in glass brick, bas relief palm trees and mermaids.

"It says the Andrea," LaBrava said, "and the Della Robbia."

"No, it don't say *the* Andrea and *the* Della Robbia." Maurice held onto LaBrava's arm, pointing now. "Read it."

"It's too dark."

"I can see it you can see it. Look. You read it straight across it says Andrea Della Robbia. He was a famous Italian sculptor back, I don't know, the fourteen, fifteen hundreds. They name these places the Esther, the Dorothy—what kind of name is that for a hotel on South Miami Beach? I mean back then. Now it don't matter. South Bronx south, it's getting almost as bad."

"Della Robbia," LaBrava said. "It's a nice name. We going?"

"You say it, Della Robbia," Maurice said, rolling the name with a soft, Mediterranean flourish, tasting it on his tongue, the sound giving him pleasure. "Then the son of a bitch I sold it to—how do you like this guy? He paints the Andrea all white, changes the style of the lettering and ruins the composition. See, both hotels before were a nice pale yellow, dark green letters, dark green the decoration parts, the names read together like they were suppose to."

16

LaBrava said, "You think anybody ever looks up there?"

"Forget I told you," Maurice said. They walked back to the car and he stopped again before getting in. "Wait. I want to take a camera with us."

"It's in the trunk."

"Which one?"

"The Leica CL."

"And a flash?"

"In the case."

Maurice paused. "You gonna wear that shirt, uh?"

LaBrava's white shirt bore a pattern of bananas, pineapples and oranges. "It's brand new, first time I've had it on."

"Got all dressed up. Who you suppose to be, Murf the Surf?"

There was a discussion when LaBrava went around the block from Ocean Drive to Collins and headed south to Fifth Street to get on the MacArthur Causeway. Maurice said, we're going north, what do you want to go south for? Why didn't you go up to Forty-first Street, take the Julia Tuttle? LaBrava said, because there's traffic up there on the beach, it's still the season. Maurice said, eleven o'clock at night? You talk about traffic, it's nothing what it used to be like. You could've gone up, taken the Seventy-ninth Street Causeway. LaBrava said, "You want to drive or you want me to?"

They didn't get too far on I-95 before they came to

all four lanes backed up, approaching the 112 inter-
change, brake lights popping on and off as far ahead
as they could see. Crawling along in low gear, stopping,
starting, the Mercedes stalled twice.

LaBrava said, "All the money you got, why don't
you buy a new car?"

Maurice said, "You know what you're talking about?
This car's a classic, collector's model."

"Then you oughta get a tune."

Maurice said, "What do you mean, all the money I
got?"

"You told me you were a millionaire one time."

"Used to be," Maurice said. "I spent most of my
dough on booze, broads and boats and the rest I
wasted."

Neither of them spoke again until they were beyond
Fort Lauderdale. They could sit without talking and
LaBrava would be reasonably comfortable; he never
felt the need to invent conversation. He was curious
when he asked Maurice:

"What do you want the camera for?"

"Maybe I want to take a picture."

"The woman?"

"Maybe. I don't know yet. I have to see how she is."

"She's a good friend of yours?"

Maurice said, "I'm going out this time of night to
help somebody I don't know? She's a very close friend."

"How come if she lives in Boca they took her to
Delray Beach?"

"That's where the place is they take them. It's run by the county. Palm Beach."

"Is it like a hospital?"

"What're you asking me for? I never been there."

"Well, what'd the girl say on the phone?"

"Something about she was brought in on the Meyers Act."

"It means she was drunk."

"That's what I'm afraid of."

"They pick you up in this state on a Meyers Act," LaBrava said, "it means you're weaving around with one eye closed, smashed. They pick you up on a Baker Act it means you're acting weird in public and're probably psycho. I remember that from when I was here before."

He had spent a year and a half in the Miami field office of the United States Secret Service, one of five different duty assignments in nine years.

He had told Maurice about it one Saturday morning driving down to Islamorada, LaBrava wanting to try bonefishing and Maurice wanting to show him where he was standing when the tidal wave hit in '35. LaBrava would remember the trip as the only time Maurice ever asked him questions, ever expressed an interest in his past life. In parts of it, anyway.

He didn't get to tell much of the IRS part, the three years he'd worked as an investigator when he was young and eager. "Young and dumb," Maurice said. Maurice didn't want to hear anything about the fucking IRS.

Or much about LaBrava's marriage, either—during the same three years—to the girl he'd met in accounting class, Wayne State University, who didn't like to drink, smoke or stay out late, or go to the show. Though she seemed to like all those things before. Strange? Her name was Lorraine. Maurice said, what's strange about it? They never turn out like you think they're going to. Skip that part. There wasn't anything anybody could tell him about married life he didn't know. Get to the Secret Service part.

Well, there was the training at Beltsville, Maryland. He learned how to shoot a Smith & Wesson .357 Magnum, the M-16, the Uzi submachine gun, different other ones. He learned how to disarm and theoretically beat the shit out of would-be assassins with a few chops and kicks. He learned how to keep his head up and his eyes open, how to sweep a crowd looking for funny moves, hands holding packages, umbrellas on clear days, that kind of thing.

He spent fifteen months in Detroit, his hometown, chasing down counterfeiters, going undercover to get next to wholesalers. That part was okay, making buys as a passer. But then he'd have to testify against the poor bastard in federal court, take the stand and watch the guy's face drop—Christ, seeing his new buddy putting the stuff on him. So once he was hot in Detroit, a familiar face in the trade, they had to send him out to cool off.

He was assigned to the Protective Research Section in Washington where, LaBrava said, he read nasty letters all day. Letters addressed to "Peanut Head Carter, the Mushmouth Motherfucker from Georgia." Or that ever-popular salutation, "To the Nigger-loving President of the Jewnited States." Letters told what should be done to the President of the USA, "the Utmost Supreme Assholes" who believed his lies. There was a suggestion, LaBrava said, the President ought to be "pierced with the prophet's sword of righteousness for being a goddamn hypocrite." Fiery, but not as practical as the one that suggested, "They ought to tie you to one of those MX missiles you dig so much and lose your war-lovin ass."

Maurice said, "People enjoy writing letters, don't they? You answer them?"

LaBrava said usually there wasn't a return address; but they'd trace the writers down through postmarks, broken typewriter keys, different clues, and have a look at them. They'd be interviewed and their names added to a file of some forty thousand presidential pen pals, a lot of cuckoos; a few, about a hundred or so, they'd have to watch.

LaBrava told how he'd guarded important people, Teddy Kennedy during the Senator's 1980 presidential campaign, trained to be steely-eyed, learned to lean away from those waving arms, stretched his steely eyes open till they ached listening to those tiresome, oh my, those boring goddamn speeches.

Maurice said, "You should a heard William Jennings Bryan, the Peerless Prince of Platform English, Christ, lecture on the wonders of Florida—sure, brought in by the real estate people."

LaBrava said he'd almost quit after guarding Teddy.

But he hung on and was reassigned to go after counterfeiters again, now out of the Miami field office, now
getting into his work and enjoying it. A new angle. He
picked up a Nikon, attached a 200-mm lens, and began
using it in surveillance work. Loved it. Snapping undercover agents making deals with wholesalers, passers
unloading their funny money. Off duty he continued
snapping away: shooting up and down Southwest
Eighth Street, the heart of Little Havana; or riding
with a couple of Metro cops to document basic Dade
County violence. He felt himself attracted to street
life. It was a strange feeling, he was at home, knew the
people; saw more outcast faces and attitudes than he
would ever be able to record, people who showed him
their essence behind all kinds of poses—did Maurice
understand this?—and trapped them in his camera for
all time.

He got hot again through court appearances and was
given a cooling-off assignment—are you ready for this?
—in Independence, Missouri.

After counterfeiters?

No, to guard Mrs. Truman.

A member of the twelve-man protective detail. To
sit in the surveillance house watching monitors or sit
eight hours a day in the Truman house itself on North
Delaware. Sit sometimes in the living room looking
around at presidential memorabilia, a picture of Mar-
garet and her two kids, the grandfather's clock that had
been wired and you didn't have to wind—which would
have been something to do—listening to faint voices
in other rooms. Or sit in the side parlor with Harry's

piano, watching movies on TV, waiting for the one interruption of the day. The arrival of the mailman.

"Don't get me wrong, Mrs. Truman was a kind, considerate woman. I liked her a lot."

The duty chief had said, "Look, there're guys would give an arm and a leg for this assignment. If you can't take pride in it, just say so."

He glanced at Maurice sitting there prim, very serious this evening. Little Maurice Zola, born here before there were roads other than a few dirt tracks and the Florida East Coast Railway. Natty little guy staring at this illuminated interstate highway—giant lit-up green signs every few miles telling where you were—and not too impressed. He had seen swamps become cities, a bridge extended to a strip of mangrove in the Atlantic Ocean and Miami Beach was born. Changes were no longer events in his life. They had happened or they didn't.

One of the green signs, mounted high, told them Daytona Beach was 215 miles.

"Who cares?" Maurice said. "I used to live in Daytona Beach. First time I got married, October 10, 1929 —wonderful time to get married, Jesus—was in Miami. The second time was October 24, 1943, in Daytona Beach. October's a bad month for me. I paid alimony, I mean plenty, but I outlived 'em both. Miserable women. In '32, when I worked for the septic tank outfit and wrestled alligators on the weekends? It was because I had the experience being married to my first wife."

"What about the lady we're going to see?"

"What about her?"

"You ever serious with her?"

"You're asking, you want to know did I go to bed with her? She wasn't that kind of girl. She wasn't a broad you did that with."

"I mean did you ever think of marrying her?"

"She was too young for me. I don't mean she was too young you wanted to hop in the sack with a broad her age, I mean to get married and live with. I had all kinds of broads at that time. In fact, go back a few years before that, just before Kefauver, when I had the photo concessions and the horse book operation. I'll tell you a secret. You want to know who one of the broads I was getting into her pants was at the time. Evelyn, at the gallery. She was in love with me."

"I don't think you've introduced me to any who weren't."

"What can I say?" Maurice said.

"How old's the woman we're going to see?"

"Jeanie? She's not too old. Lemme think, it was '58 I gave her a piece of the hotel. Or it might've been '59, they were making that movie on the beach. Frank Sinatra, Edward G. Robinson . . . Jeanie was gonna be in the picture, was why she came down. But she didn't get the part."

"Wait a minute—" LaBrava said.

"They wanted her, but then they decided she looked too young. She was in her twenties then and she was gonna play this society woman."

"Jeanie—"

"Yeah, very good-looking girl, lot of class. She married a guy—not long after that she married a guy she met down here. Lawyer, very wealthy, use to represent some of the big hotels. They had a house on Pine Tree Drive, I mean a mansion, faced the Eden Roc across Indian Creek. You know where I mean? Right in there, by Arthur Godfrey Road. Then Jerry, Jerry Breen was the guy's name, had some trouble with the IRS, had to sell the place. I don't know if it was tax fraud or what. He didn't go to jail, anything like that, but it cost him, I'll tell you. He died about oh, ten years ago. Yeah, Jeanie was a movie actress. They got married she retired, gave it up."

"What was her name before?"

"Just lately I got a feeling something funny's going on. She call me last week, start talking about she's got some kind of problem, then changes the subject. I don't know if she means with the booze or what."

"You say she was a movie actress."

"She was a star. You see her on TV once in a while, they show the old movies."

"Her name Jeanie or Jean?"

"Jean. Jean—the hell was her name? You believe it? I'm used to thinking of her as Jeanie Breen." Maurice pointed. "Atlantic Boulevard. See it? Mile and a half. You better get over." Maurice rolled his window down.

"Jean Simmons?"

"Naw, not Jean Simmons." Maurice was half-turned now, watching for cars coming up in the inside lane. "I'll tell you when."

"Gene Tierney?" *Laura.* He'd watched it on television in Bess Truman's living room. "How's she spell her name?"

"Jean. How do you spell Jean? J-e-a-n."

Jean Harlow was dead. LaBrava looked at the rearview mirror, watched headlights lagging behind, in no hurry. "Jeanne Crain?"

"Naw, not Jeanne Crain. Get ready," Maurice said. "Not after this car but the one after it, I think you can make it."

Commentary on *LaBrava*

ELMORE LEONARD

The best time to begin writing a novel is when you least expect to. Otherwise you can prepare forever, plotting, researching, getting to know your characters —putting it off is what you're doing—to the point that the act of beginning becomes a major event, if not a psychological hang-up.

On December 24, 1982, at about three in the afternoon—during a lull in preparation for Christmas Eve —and without giving it much thought, I began writing *LaBrava*. By five o'clock I was 2½ pages into a book I would be working on for the next four months at least, or until I had written between 350 and 400 manuscript pages. (The length isn't planned; that's simply the way it comes out.) I felt good about the 2½ pages in that I liked the sound, the attitudes of the two characters I had introduced, and also because I was now, unexpectedly, on my way—a week earlier than I had originally planned to begin.

" 'I'm going to tell you a secret I never told anybody around here,' Maurice said. . . ."

In that Christmas Eve opening Maurice Zola and Joe LaBrava come out of an old South Miami Beach hotel called the Della Robbia, and I began to hear them: Maurice—a talker, an opinionated old guy; LaBrava—quiet, patient up to a point. A woman is mentioned, "The lady we're gonna rescue. . . ." They get in Maurice's old-model Mercedes and drive off.

The opening of a book may or may not hold up under subsequent revisions. Within the next few weeks I wrote a new opening chapter to focus directly on LaBrava and identify him through his work as a street photographer; that is, by looking at the kinds of photos he takes. The Christmas Eve pages were then used to open chapter 2, reprinted here, and did survive pretty much as they were written. Maurice's describing how you could always spot a bookie in the old days was added later; so were the Yiddish words in reference to the old ladies who live in the hotel. It's like adding a pinch of this and a pinch of that: seasoning that's thrown in while the story is cooking.

My main concern in this sequence, as it continued, was how to work in LaBrava's background as a Secret Service agent. Driving along with Maurice seemed an appropriate time to do it, if I could pull it off without interrupting the sound and continuity of the story. So I referred to another time: "He had told Maurice about it one Saturday morning driving down to Isla-morada . . ." presented his Secret Service history in a somewhat conversational manner, and this way maintained the tone of the scene, two men riding in a car together talking.

But even after I'd finished the book, I was concerned. I felt that the story didn't reach its first dramatic conflict quickly enough, the plot developing too leisurely, and that it was the description of LaBrava's background, though only three pages, that was causing the problem.

I asked my publisher, Don Fine, about it, and he said, "That works okay. You need it there; it's your first chapter that's too long." I had my doubts. But I cut seven pages from the original thirteen, and that was it. Amazing. The pace of the entire book seemed to pick up.

Right now I'm planning another book, assembling characters and settings, gathering research material, gradually closing in on that day when, quite unexpectedly, I'll begin to write.

I can hardly wait.

George Smiley
Goes Home

JOHN LE CARRÉ

John le Carré has established the standard by which contemporary novels of international intrigue are measured. The chief character in six of his ten novels is George Smiley, the aging master spy for the British Secret Service who is also the subject of this television sketch written to set up his character for viewers of a 1977 BBC program on le Carré. "George Smiley Goes Home" was published in The Bell House Book *(1979), a volume commemorating the John Farquharson literary agency. This is the first publication in America.*

John le Carré is the pseudonym of David Cornwell, a former British Foreign Servant. From 1960 to 1963, he was second secretary in the British Embassy in Bonn. In 1964 he served as consul in Hamburg. His eleventh novel is to be published in spring 1986.

INTERIOR. A laundry and drycleaning business in the King's Road, Chelsea, DAY.

A fogged picture slowly hardens, as the steady, near-expressionless monologue of a cockney working woman grinds on. It is the voice of LILY, the shop manageress, a dumpy, crippled little woman in a rabbit jacket. She is talking, near enough to herself, supplying background music to her own actions as she accepts the customers' tickets, limps to one rack or the other, stands on a stool or uses a steel grappler in order to fetch down a brown paper parcel or a peg-full of dry cleaning.

Still talking, she takes the money, rings up the change, turns to the next customer, receives a fresh supply of dirty clothes. The shop is busy and she deals with the shifting knot of customers expertly. Among them is George SMILEY, and though he is already near the counter, there is unobtrusive comedy in the way he constantly allows himself to be bypassed by less diffi-dent customers. He holds out his ticket, almost gets LILY to take it—only at the last moment to see him-self supplanted.

SMILEY is late fifties, bespectacled, fat, shy- ʼκ ng. He wears a dark suit.

LILY
(busy all the time)
... I don't like youth. I'm not saying anything about young people—(fetches down a parcel) —we were all young once—laundry or dry, dear?—We all missed our chances, I dare say, or took them and lived to regret it—(to an-other customer)—Done your list, have you? In the basket then, that's the way—They don't *do* anything, they don't want to work, they're half dead, same as my nephew. I said to his mother —(taking a ticket)—name, dear?

31

Eldridge.

LILY
(pulling down a parcel)
—"give him everything he wants," I said, "but
don't *spoil* him. If you spoil him he'll turn to
crime, *then* where will he be?" Gives him an
electric guitar for his Christmas, all her savings
and half next year's. Still it's what she wants,
you can't stop them. Name, dear?

SMILEY
(as LILY takes his ticket)
Smiley. George Smiley.

LILY
(studying ticket)
You want to learn to stand up for yourself,
darling, don't you. I like "George." I always
said I'd *have* had a George, if I'd had one.
Which is it, dear?

SMILEY
I'm sorry?

LILY
Laundry or dry, dear?

SMILEY
Oh laundry. Yes, laundry.

Turning her back on him, LILY peers up into the shelves, as she continues her flat monologue.

Hey-diddle-dee, where can you *be*? (Starts climbing a ladder, grapple in hand) How long ago, darling, remember?

SMILEY

Last October. The twenty-ninth. A Thursday.
Reaching, LILY turns and peers down at him. Beat.

LILY

What are you, brain of Britain?

SMILEY

No, no, it was just the day she left . . . for the country . . . (repeats) Smiley . . .

LILY

(still searching)
. . . That's the most important thing in life. Smile. They ask me at the training course. Lily, they say, what's the most important thing?—(as she takes down parcels, examines labels, returns them)—Give them a smile, I say. I had a bloke walk in yesterday, no class but chivalrous. He said to me "that's the first smile I've seen all week." (She takes down another parcel and stares at the label, then at SMILEY, seeming somehow to compare them. Finally:) What's your address, then, dear?

33

SMILEY

Bywater Street.

LILY
(still unsatisfied)
What number, darling?

SMILEY

Nine. Nine, Bywater Street.
With a shrug, LILY starts down the ladder.

LILY

It says *"Lady Ann* Smiley."

SMILEY

That's my wife. She's away.

LILY
(approaching till)
You a lord then?

SMILEY

No, no. She is. I mean she's the daughter of
one.

LILY

What does that make you, then? (Rings up
two pounds eighty, takes his money, turns to
the next customer) Laundry or dry, dear? In
the basket then, that's the way . . .

34

SMILEY

(as he takes his change and escapes)

Excuse me ... good day ... thank you ...

Ae he exits, we hear LILY's voice, to the other customers, droning on.

LILY

(as we dissolve)

I remember her, see? That's why I was suspicious. Beauty and brains, they're like oil and
water, that's what I say.

We have long DISSOLVED over LILY's voice to:
EXT. KING's ROAD DAY, and are following SMILEY
as he walks, laundry parcel under his arm, along the
pavement, past swinging shoppers to the turning
marked "Bywater Street." He enters it.
NEW ANGLE, SMILEY's POV.
Bywater Street is a cul-de-sac. We follow SMILEY past
the parked cars.
NEW ANGLE, showing the door of Number Nine,
Bywater Street. One full milk bottle on the doorstep.
SMILEY still has the parcel under his arm as he moves
up the steps to his own front door. He is at the top
step when:
CLOSE on SMILEY. Nothing dramatic, almost nothing
at all. But a momentary hardening of his expression.
CLOSE on the lower window. Did we see a shadow?
Did SMILEY? Is the net curtain very slightly moving?
CLOSE on SMILEY. He holds his own front door key
in his hand. Transferring his gaze from the window, he
looks downward, at his feet.

NEW ANGLE, SMILEY's POV. At SMILEY's feet, a tiny wedge of wood lies on the doorstep, where it has fallen from its place in the lintel.

NEW ANGLE. The door in CLOSE-UP, showing the two sturdy Banham deadlocks. Reaching up, SMILEY very quickly runs his hand along the lintel, confirming his suspicion that the wedge is no longer in place.

CLOSE on SMILEY as he discreetly drops the door key back into his pocket. Then, without further hesitation, he presses his own front door bell.

HOLD SMILEY as he waits impassively, the parcel under his arm. From inside the house, footsteps approach.

We HEAR the sound of a chain being unlatched.

ANOTHER ANGLE, over SMILEY's shoulder, to show life continuing perfectly normally in the street. A mother pushes her pram, a lonely queer exercises his dog, the milkman continues his round.

ANOTHER ANGLE as the door brightly opens, showing: A tall, fair, handsome thirty-five-year-old man, dressed in a light grey suit and silver tie. Scandinavian or German. Could be a diplomat. His left hand nonchalantly in his jacket pocket.

> STRANGER
> (German accent)

Good morning.

> SMILEY

Oh. Good morning. I'm sorry to bother you.

Not at all. How can I help you?

SMILEY

Is Mr. Smiley in, please? Mr. George Smiley? My name is Mackie, I live round the corner. He does know me.

STRANGER

George is upstairs just at the moment. I am a friend of his, just visiting. Won't you come in?

SMILEY

No, no, it's not necessary. If you'd give him this. (He takes the parcel, hands it to him.) Mackie, Bill Mackie. He asked me to pick it up for him.

Ignoring the parcel, the STRANGER opens the door still wider.

STRANGER

But I'm sure he would like to see you for a moment!
(He calls into the house)
George! Bill Mackie is here. Come down! He has not been well, you see. He loves to be visited. But today he is up at last, such a joy.
(Back to SMILEY)
There, I can hear him coming now. Please come in. You know how he is about the cold.

37

SMILEY
(dumping the parcel into the STRANGER's one
free arm)
Thanks, but I must be getting along.

EXT. BYWATER STREET. SMILEY making briskly
along the pavement, away from his house, towards the
King's Road. As he walks, CLOSE fast on successive
car numbers, aerials, wing mirrors, etc. SMILEY's expression impassive, functional, not a backward glance.
Track him round the corner, into the King's Road,
along the pavement towards a line of phones, most of
them smashed.

INT. a filthy phone box. SMILEY talking into the phone.

SMILEY
. . . height five eleven, colour of eyes blue,
colour of hair light brown, youthful hairline,
powerful build, clean shaven, German accent,
northern at a guess, possibly left handed. Two
unfamiliar cars parked in the street, GRK 117F,
black Ford van, no rear windows, two aerials,
two wing mirrors, looks like an old surveillance
horse. OAR 289G, green Datsun saloon with
scratch marks on the offside rear wing, could
be hired. Both empty, but the Datsun had
today's *Evening Standard* on the driving seat,
late edition. They're to wait till he leaves, then
house him, that's all. Two teams and ring the
changes all the time. A lace-curtain job. No
branch lines, no frightening the game. Tell
Toby.

(So far, he has a deadpan expression. Now his manner
is torn between fear for his wife and plain anger.)
And then, Peter . . . ring Ann for me, will you.
Tell her that if by any chance she was thinking
of coming back to the house in the next few
days—*don't.*

Come Morning

JOE GORES

Joe Gores was the first writer to win Edgar Allan Poe awards in three categories: for the best first mystery novel, A Time of Predators, in 1969; for the best mystery story, "Goodbye, Pops," in 1969; and for the best episode in a television dramatic series, "No Immunity for Murder" on Kojak, in 1975. Before turning to a literary career, Gores worked at what he regards as the related occupation of private investigator: "A detective gets in and digs around in the garbage of people's lives. A novelist invents people and then digs around in their garbage. They are very similar."

Gores is currently working on a new novel and episodic television scripts. Come Morning, the novel from which this excerpt is taken, will be published in spring 1986 by the Mysterious Press.

WHEN RUNYAN was captured eight years be-*fore, the $2,000,000 in diamonds he stole were not recovered. As a result, upon his parole from San Quentin, he finds his freedom and his life threatened on every side: by the insurance investigator who arranged his parole, by mysterious former "partners" who want their cut, by an unknown killer who wants him dead.*

plans to get the diamonds from where he hid them and buy his way out. But they are gone. Now his only hope is to pull another robbery—something he swore never to do again—and use the proceeds to stay alive.

"Brother Blood's out making a coke buy," said Taps. He was a handsome ebony man of about thirty-three, with some of Eddie Murphy's sly, jive-ass manner. "You got one hour for sure, maybe more."

It was 1:21 in the morning. As they passed the Sunset Boulevard exit of the San Diego Freeway, Grace got the rented Cougar into the right lane. Traffic was late-night fast but light. Louise was beside her in the front seat; Taps and Runyan were in the back. The night was clear and dark and crisp.

"An hour's enough." Runyan fought to keep irritation out of his voice. Pregame tension.

"I hear you talkin'." Tension strummed Taps's voice also.

They must have gone over the plan in broad strokes a hundred, two hundred times in San Quentin, a fantasy scheme to pass a few of the endless prison hours. Now it was happening.

Grace took the Wilshire Boulevard exit, following the off ramp down and around under the freeway past the huge sterile landscaped area of the Los Angeles Veterans Administration. She went east on Wilshire.

They passed the anachronistic one-story, red-roofed Ships Restaurant in Westwood, a gaudy soft palate for the new high-rise condo teeth that lined Wilshire like multimillion-dollar inlays; a half-mile beyond, Grace turned off at the fringes of the ultraprivate L.A. Country Club.

She turned again, then slowed to crawl past a pair of high-rise condos that took up an entire block. She was a very beautiful black woman in her twenties who wore her hair natural and very short.

"Brother Blood's penthouse is in the one on the right."

"You go in the one on the left," added Taps unnecessarily. "Not so much security."

Runyan didn't say anything at all. He wished Taps hadn't come up with that idea about not leaving the penthouse with the bonds. He desperately wanted it not to mean the obvious but knew he was going to have to find out the hard way. He was five years older than Taps, with shiny black prison-chopped hair and piercing blue eyes.

Grace turned right at the next corner, then right again and stopped. They were now around behind the buildings. Runyan took a deep silent breath, gripped his black nylon stuff bag, and opened his door.

"Twelve minutes," he told the back of Grace's head as he stepped out into the street.

Without turning, she said, "I'll be ready."

Runyan closed his door without slamming it, went around behind the back of the waiting car to the curb side. Although the street was residential-area deserted, he could hear occasional cars on Wilshire two blocks away.

Louise reached a hand out of her window. When he took it, her skin was warm, almost hot, as if she were slightly feverish. She was twenty-nine, the most beautiful woman Runyan had ever known, with shoulder-length black hair and a sensual face.

"Eight years," Runyan said with a nervous grin. Eight years in the belly of the beast.

"Eight years better," said Louise. Her wide-set emerald eyes, which seemed to glow with an inner light, caught and held his gaze.

Runyan nodded, suddenly jaunty; his jitters had disappeared when she had spoken. Taps stuck his head and one arm out of the rear window; the manicured nail of his long brown forefinger made tiny ticking noises against the crystal of his watch.

"The power goes off fifteen minutes after Grace goes in. Then you got ninety seconds to get on and off the cable, or—"

"Or I fry," said Runyan.

"And remember Brother Blood owns the damn building, so when you've made the switch—"

"I know what to do," Runyan said flatly.

Grace drove aimlessly to kill the minutes ber   went in. Taps leaned his forearms on the back o. ..e front seat, his head behind and between those of the two women in front of him.

"We got a couple minutes for insurance. Swing by the dealer's an' make sure Brother Blood is where he's s'pozed to be."

They crossed Beverly Glen on Lindbrook, and near Holmby drove by a long black Mercedes limo with a middle-aged black chauffeur leaning against the front fender and smoking a fat brown cigar.

"Yeah!" exclaimed Taps. "We're on!"

Grace drove the Cougar back the way she had come and stopped on a side street a block from the condos. Taps got out; he wore work clothes and a Dodgers souvenir baseball cap. He carried an electrician's black metal toolbox.

"You got five minutes," he warned Grace.

"I be late, shugah," she drawled, "you fire my ass."

Taps watched the car drive away. It was all expensive homes here, in the multihundred-thousand-dollar range. Pool man on Mondays, wetback Mexican gardeners on Wednesdays, private school for the kids, vacation in Puerto Vallarta with Europe every third year. Well, his turn now.

He walked quickly back to a manhole cover flush with the concrete, took a stubby wrecking bar out from under his windbreaker, inserted the bent end into the socket, and heaved the cover aside. It grated loudly in the still night air. He sat down on the edge, found the ladder with his toes, shot another look around, then went down out of sight. The cover grated back, clanging dully into place. The street was deserted again.

Grace had parked the Cougar in midblock so that it wasn't really in front of either high rise. Louise, leaned back against the locked door on her side of the car, watched Grace use the tipped-down rearview mirror to make herself into a whore. Grace caught her eye in the mirror and winked.

"Your man's gonna be just fine, honey."

"I thought you didn't like him," said Louise coldly. "Said he was trouble."

From a handbag big enough to hold an UZI machine gun, Grace took purple three-inch spikes and a bright purple silk scarf. She cinched the scarf tight around her middle, leaving the ends hanging over one hip. Then she jerked the zipper of her shimmery red jumpsuit down almost to her navel.

"I like you and him together, shugah," she drawled. "You go by your gut feelin' with a man, you don't never be wrong."

She wore no brassiere; her breasts were magnificent, bared almost to the edge of the areolas, but she frowned down at them, then began rolling her nipples between her fingers and thumbs until they stood out boldly against the thin satin material.

Finally she looked over at Louise. "How do I look?"

"Like a two-dollar quickie on the back seat."

Grace winked again. "You got it, shugah."

She opened her door and got out. Louise slid over under the wheel. She had always considered herself quite sophisticated; Grace made her feel young and naive as a virgin.

She called, "Good luck."

Grace turned and gave her a street urchin's grin and a thumbs-up signal, then cut at an angle across the carefully barbered and lit lawn toward the front entrance of the condo that did not have Brother Blood's penthouse perched on top of it.

Picking any lock takes a certain amount of time and a great deal of skill. It is not the simple matter that television would have us believe. Nobody ever picked a lock with one pick; at the outset a tension tool—an L-shaped piece of spring steel—must be inserted into the keyhole and turned slightly so that as you raise each pin to its shear line, the tension will keep it from falling back down into the core.

Runyan had spent 2.5 minutes trying to "rake" the lock of the basement rear service entrance of the high rise—the quick and easy way that sometimes works in a matter of seconds—then had gotten serious: another 7.55 minutes with his tension tool and a curved-tip pick before the lock finally yielded.

He made no move to open the door, instead held it just fractionally ajar; he knew that a closed-circuit TV scanning camera was covering the inside of it. He checked the luminous dial of his watch: less than a minute to go.

Emery Samnic was forty-seven years old, had been married to the same woman for twenty-six years, and despite this—or because of it—had his sexual fantasies like any other man. For five nights a week he wore the uniform of a security guard and sat behind the security desk in the high-rise lobby.

It was good duty. Tipped back in his swivel chair,

he had only to turn his head to examine the bank of TV-screen monitors set against the back of the security cubicle. The monitors covered the condo's entrances, doorways, corridors, and the interiors of the elevators. In one a guard walked a hallway; the others showed nothing at all.

A beautiful black woman appeared in the front-entrance monitor to push the night buzzer. It sounded behind Emery's desk. She waited with a hip thrust out provocatively, her big gaudy handbag tucked under one arm, tapping a three-inch spike against the pavement, a thin brown cigar between her lips.

There was no one else with her, but Emery stood up and loosened the Smith & Wesson .38 police special in his belt holster before pushing the button to release the door catch.

On the screen, the black woman opened the door and disappeared. The real Grace, in living color, simultaneously came across the lobby toward his desk, her heels clop-clopping on the terrazzo, everything moving the way women's bodies moved in his fantasies. Her expression was go-to-hell, and she obviously wore no bra or panties under the clinging red jumpsuit.

Emery cleared his throat and said, "This isn't your sort of place, sister."

Grace put her elbows on his counter, thrusting out her butt and languidly blowing smoke in his face.

"I is *in*vited, honey." She had a slightly husky voice.

She could see past Emery's thick waist to the basement monitor. Runyan opened the loading door and entered boldly. She leaned closer yet, giving Emery the news all the way to her navel. As Runyan walked over to the freight elevator and pushed the button, Grace pointed at the house phone with a very long synthetic purple nail.

"Why don't you phone up the man and find out? Apartment . . . two three seven."

What sort of business would the Rotzels have with this sort of woman at almost two in the morning? The old man was a deacon of the Baptist church, for Pete's sake.

"This time of night . . ." Emery began, letting it hang.

Grace moved her cleavage closer; across the lobby, the elevator indicator glowed as the cage descended to Runyan.

"It was a *urgent* phone call, shugah," she said. "I swear I think that man was watching a dirty movie, and he's got his *motor* running, you know what I mean. . . ."

Emery knew what she meant: he could feel his dork pushing out against the heavy twill uniform pants. Jesus, what would it be like to put the old banana into something like that?

He unconsciously blew out a deep breath and picked up the house phone and tapped out two three seven. On the monitors, the elevator door opened and Runyan stepped through, disappearing from the basement screen to be instantly picked up by the adjacent elevator camera. Grace could hear an angry squawking voice on the phone. Hurry, Runyan, damn you!

Emery said unhappily into the phone, "This is Emery on the lobby desk downstairs. I'm sorry to disturb you, sir, but there's a young lady here who says—" He broke off to listen to more squawks, finally said, "I know what time it is, sir, I surely do, but she says you wanted—"

Grace, watching Runyan spring up and knock open the elevator ceiling trap, reached across the counter to grab the phone out of Emery's hand.

"Lemme talk to him," she said, then said into the phone, "Listen, buster, you phone up an say you needs an around the world, *bad.* Now what's this shit about—"

"Who *is* this?" demanded a high scratchy man's voice. "How *dare* you use language like that to me? My wife and I are Christian people who—"

"So you got your old lady there; so I takes care of her too," said Grace, winking at the openmouthed Emery. "All it'll cost you is an extra fifty—"

"I'm going to call the police and report you!" shrieked the man on the phone. On the monitor, Runyan was tossing his stuff bag up through the ceiling trap. In front of her, Emery was starting to turn toward the monitors. Grace quickly thrust the phone back into his hands.

"Man wanta talk to you."

On the monitor, Runyan crouched for his leap.

On the phone, the confused Emery said, "I . . . I'm real sorry, Mr. Rotzel, I didn't know she was going to—"

"*Rotzel?*"

Grace reached over and broke the connection in midword. Behind Emery, Runyan leaped up and grabbed the edges of the trap.

"Rotzel ain't the name of the dude phone up! What's this here address?"

"Uh . . . twelve forty-two Bonington—"

"*Sheeit*, shugah, I got the wrong building!"

Grace winked at Emery and swiveled her way toward the door, her exaggerated hip swing holding his lusting eyes long enough for Runyan to disappear through the trap in the elevator ceiling. As the door closed behind Grace, Emery wiped the sheen of sweat from his forehead and whirled belatedly to check the monitors. Everything was serene, nothing moving anywhere.

Standing on the roof of the elevator cage, Runyan took a pair of odd-looking clamplike things called Jumar ascenders from his black nylon stuff bag and fitted them to the cable about eighteen inches apart. They had rope slings that hung about three feet below them. The clock was really running now. Runyan put his feet in the slings and, stuff bag clipped to his belt, began walking himself up the cable.

Under the street two blocks away, Taps Turner was moving cautiously along one of the utility access tunnels by the light of a tiny powerful halogen-bulb flashlight. He set down his electrician's kit in front of a switch box bolted to one wall and used his pry bar to break the padlock hasp. Inside the hinged cover were rows of engaged knife switches. He began to compare the interior layout of the box with a wiring diagram, humming a Lionel Richie love ballad softly under his breath.

Louise drove the Cougar while, beside her, Grace wiped the makeup off her face with a wad of Kleenex. Both women were laughing at her tale of Emery's wandering eyes and bulging pants.

In the elevator shaft, Runyan grunted his way upward. The air was close and smelled of hot metal and lubricating oil. Runyan's movements were crisp, executed without hesitation. He had to be exact because he had no "protection" in place—he was working without a safety line. The strength of his grip on the Jumars and the sureness of his feet in the slings were his only insurance against falling as he practiced this mild form of . . . what? Masochism? Maybe self-abuse. His body was sure feeling abused as he used the Jumars to climb the cable.

Endlessly.

He rested a moment, panting, tipped his head back to look up into the dimness of the shaft. The big wheels over which the cables ran still seemed a long way up.

He went into the fugue state he had perfected while practicing gymnastics at Q, trying to pass the endless hours of confinement. One of the prison survival skills you never heard about was infinite patience. He had learned it.

What was Louise doing right now? He checked his watch. Still driving around; she wouldn't park the car near the other condo's underground-garage entrance until about five minutes before he was scheduled to be coming out.

He shoved a Jumar up the cable, and it rapped against the rim of the grooved wheel over which the cable passed.

He'd made it!

Runyan grabbed the nearest spoke of the wheel, made sure of his grip, then carefully disengaged his feet from the Jumar slings to swing his legs up and hook them around the wheel rim.

Hanging backward under it like a sloth under a branch, he removed the Jumars from the cable with his free hand, clipped them to carabiners threaded on his belt. Then he merely climbed the spokes of the massive wheel so he could step onto the metal grid-work service platform.

The housing door, as on the diagram he had studied, opened out onto the blacktopped roof of the building. He stopped for a few moments, massaging tautness from his arms while gulping fresh night air. Still on time, he negotiated the mini–obstacle course of capped chimneys and vents toward the edge of the building that faced the twin high rise a hundred feet away.

On the inside of the four-foot-high concrete parapet was a sign held to the wall with cement screws: DANGER —HIGH TENSION. He bent across the top of the low wall to look down.

Bingo. A very thick black power cable ran along the outside of the building five feet below, did a right angle through a terminal box, and stretched away into the darkness toward Brother Blood's building. Right where it was supposed to be.

Runyan checked his watch again, unclipped the stuff bag from his belt, set it on the roof, and took out one of the climbers' lights known as break-'em-shake-'ems. He bent it into a horseshoe around his neck; it glowed with a soft cool green light like Darth Vader's sword. Break-'em-shake-'ems left the hands free, a vital factor in rock climbing.

He zipped the bag, clipped it back on the belt, and unclipped his Jumars. He put them on the top of the parapet, then jumped up so he was sitting on it between them, facing in.

He checked his watch again. One minute before two A.M.

Down in the utility tunnel below the street, Taps checked his watch: its digital number showed 1:59:07 and :08 and :09.

Runyan had edged himself back across the top of the wall until his butt was hanging off into space. This was the tricky part. He now was supported only by his hands gripping the outside angle of the top and the outer wall, and by his heels hooked over the inside edge.

Runyan hyperventilated, focusing his energies to

that white-hot physical point that perhaps only athletes know, then let his knees slowly bend, arching his body back and down. Now only his heels hooked over that inner edge, and his calves along the top of the wall supported his body; he was hanging face-out, upside down above the high-tension cable terminal.

He groped above him on top of the parapet for one of the Jumars, found it, brought it slowly down in front of his face. If he should drop one of them now, it was all over.

In the tunnel, Taps's glowing watch digits read 1:59:58 and :59 and 2:00:00, and his hands, in place on two of the knife switches, pulled them down to disengage them.

In the Cougar, Louise was just turning into the block where the high rises were when all the lights went out except the streetlights. She grabbed Grace's arm in her excitement.

"It's happenin,' baby, it's happenin'!" responded Grace in a voice almost guttural with tension.

Hanging upside down by the green glow of his break-'em-shake-'em, supported by his calves and heels on the parapet, Runyan jammed the first Jumar into place, squeezing it down so the brake bit into the high-tension core of the cable with its relentless grip. He knew that if the power had not been cut, he already would have been just smoking meat.

He found the second Jumar, fixed it in place. In his head, the seconds were ticking away. There were only ninety of them before Taps reengaged the knife switches.

He gripped the Jumars with his iron hands and kicked off the building. His body swung out and down and around, his arms and hands taking the full shocking jolt of his weight as he jerked up under the cable. He was now hanging from the Jumars only by his grip, which already had loosened the brakes so he was sliding down the cable toward Brother Blood's building.

Emery skittered his flashlight beam around a lobby lit only by the streetlights outside. Over by the elevators a second guard's flash danced and probed.

"It isn't just us, Emery," he called.

Emery felt a great weight lift off him. He had been afraid it might somehow have something to do with that black hooker who had showed up. "Okay, then, I'll call Water and Power," he said.

Runyan, still lit only by his break-'em-shake-'em, walked the Jumars quickly up the cable toward the junction box on Brother Blood's building, panting with the nonstop effort as the seconds exploded in his brain. At the box he reached over, a hand at a time, to grab the bare power cable. Then he kipped himself up into a full press-out. He got a foot up onto the cable, a knee, was balancing on the wire, grabbed the edge of the parapet, and jerked his feet up off the cable.

There were crackling bursts of white light as the Jumars, scorched and smoking, fell away. The lights flickered on in the buildings as he muscled himself up onto the wall and dropped over onto the roof.

He ran lightly across a patio landscaped with expensive potted greenery and shrubs to the sliding glass doors to the penthouse. It looked like a lock that might be reasonable about raking. Since the penthouse was supposedly the only way to the roof, he didn't have to worry about alarms.

Louise had pulled over to the curb and stopped when the lights had gone out. Now, ninety seconds later, they were back on again. She whirled on Grace.

"Did he make it? *Did he?*"

"I didn't see no falling bodies," smiled Grace. "Relax, shugah. That man of yours, he's a survivor." She dug an elbow into Louise's ribs. "Lets get moving again, baby. Don't wanta draw no po-leece before Taps can get out of that manhole."

With a thrust of his powerful shoulders, Taps heaved the manhole cover aside. He grabbed the tool kit from where it was wedged between him and the ladder, set it on the street, then leaped nimbly up on the pavement himself. He kicked the manhole cover, clanging, back into place, ran to the sidewalk.

He had taken only half a dozen jaunty and unconcerned steps when a Power and Water truck came rumbling around the corner and stopped beside the manhole. The uniformed workmen who got out never even glanced his way.

Runyan slid open one of the glass doors, entered, shut and locked it carefully behind him, then pushed his way through the drapes into the spacious living room. The dim glow of his break-'em-shake-'em showed it was sumptuous and decorator perfect.

The study also was a decorator's dream of a study: thick carpets, minicomputer and letter-quality printer, massive hardwood desk, overstuffed leather executive's swivel chair that looked ready to fly, waist-to-ceiling bookshelves behind the desk, silver-edged trophy plaques on the walls.

"Coke-Dealer-of-the-Year Award," muttered Runyan. He shut the door and returned his break-'em-shake-'em to the stuff bag after turning on the lights. His hour was almost up.

The telephone was a futuristic model with memory; on one side of it was a black oblong box with buttons on it, on the other a computer modem cradle for the receiver. It was the key to the safe, but here Taps's intelligence was vague. Runyan pushed the top button on the black box. The stereo deck started to play. He pushed it again. The stereo stopped.

Second button. The maple doors slid open on the huge console TV, and the set switched on. Again. Off.

Third. Lights on and off.

Fourth. Window blinds.

When Runyan pushed the fifth button, a panel of

the bookshelves, books and all, swung open to reveal a small wall safe of hardened cadmium steel. Runyan tried the swing handle. Locked. He went back to the desk and pushed the final button. Nothing happened. Again. The safe was still locked.

How would the mind of a Brother Blood work? Intricate mind. Liked games. Liked gadgets. A sly and tricky dude. . . .

He picked up the receiver and fitted it into the computer modem. Then he punched the final button again. Nothing. He flicked the black ON-OFF rocker switch on the back of the computer, tried again. The door of the safe popped open an inch.

Yeah. The games people play. Here's to you, Brother Blood. He switched off the computer and took from the stuff bag the orderly stacks of ornately scrolled counterfeit bearer bonds. Inside the safe were exactly similar stacks of genuine bearer bonds with the same sequenced serial numbers. He put these stacks on the far end of the desk. It would be disastrous to mix them up.

Taps cut off from the sidewalk between bushes to the rear wall of Brother Blood's building. He had just set down his electrician's box when a thin nylon cord set down Runyan's black nylon stuff bag a dozen feet away. Taps slashed the cord with his pocketknife and walked away with the bag, not glancing back, not bothering with his tool kit.

At the corner was one of the open pay phones without a booth. He looked quickly, almost guiltily around, then slotted his dimes and tapped out a seven-digit local number.

"Yeah," he said into the phone. "I want to talk with Brother Blood. Tell him Taps Turner is calling."

When Louise turned the corner, Taps was at the open-style booth, talking and gesturing earnestly on the pay phone. Beside her, Grace drew in a sharp breath.

"That rotten son of a bitch! Stop the car!"

She was out before it stopped moving, leaving her door hanging open and Louise gaping after her, open-mouthed, as she ran across the grass strip toward the phone where Taps was just saying, "Okay, that be cool. . . ."

Grace snatched the receiver out of his hand and slammed it back onto the hooks. He backhanded her across the face, yelping in astonishment, "You *crazy*, woman? Whuffo you—"

Grace was yelling, *"He saved your life! You owe him!"*

He grabbed her by the arms and started shaking her, barely aware of Louise's pale shocked face framed in the open car door a few yards away.

"We got the bonds, all of 'em!" Seeing some of the wildness fading from her eyes, he gingerly released his grip on Grace's arms. In a quieter voice, he said, "Wasn't no way we could do that except make sure he couldn't ever come back at us."

"You did it *'cause* he saved your ass in prison," said Grace in a low, intense voice. "There ain't a livin' soul in this world you'd do that for, an' you can't stand thinkin' about it." She gave a harsh laugh. "And now Brother Blood's gonna take you down, nigger."

Taps hesitated when, in the background, their car suddenly fishtailed away, so abruptly that Grace's open door slammed shut. He felt sudden fear. Grace wasn't hardly ever wrong; and now the white bitch Runyan had brought along had cut out with their car, stranding them. But he said, "You . . . you're crazy, woman."

"Don't you see it yet?" she asked in an almost tired voice. "Brother Blood, he's gonna start wonderin', How that man know to call me at the dealer's unless he was in on it an' just chicken out at the last minute?" Over his protestations, she continued, "It's what you'd think, was you. Ain't Brother Blood gonna be any different." She shook her head and turned away from him. "I ain't hangin' around to die with no boot dumb as you."

Taps let her get almost to the sidewalk before he called after her, *"But I got the bonds, baby!"*

She turned to look at him almost with pity. "You got shit, Taps. You think Runyan didn't know you planned to cross him when you asked he th'ow those bonds down to you?"

She trudged away, her steps tapping out a jaunty staccato in marked contrast to the slump of her shoulders. Taps wanted to run after her, grab her, make it right. But he had to know about this first. He ripped open the black stuff bag with his switchblade in a frenzy of anticipation and dread. It was full of newspapers folded to the approximate size of bearer bonds.

·   ·   ·

Runyan stepped into Brother Blood's private elevator and pushed the GARAGE button next to the LOBBY and PENTHOUSE buttons. Tight security. He touched the bulky oblong under his sweater. If Taps was waiting for him across the street from the garage entrance, then everything was straight; if not, yet another friend had betrayed him. He was running out of people who hadn't tried it, one way or another. Even Louise. . . .

Ashcan that. It was all in the past. They were together now for the long run; they could depend on each other for anything. In five minutes it would all be over.

Taps Turner had a terminal case of the stupids, thought Brother Blood. Planning to steal the bond stash—with a white dude, yet!—and then chickening out and thinking he'd be dumb enough to swallow the con about stumbling across the robbery! No, Taps was dog meat right now; he just didn't know it yet.

Brother Blood was a tall lean bald hollow-eyed man, impeccably dressed in a three-piece midnight blue suit and mirror-shined black oxfords. He leaned forward to peer out of the windshield past the beefy shoulder of his bodyguard as the black stretch limo was whispering down the deserted street beside his apartment building.

They turned the corner. The driver pushed the remote electronic-eye activator. Fifty yards away, the heavy steel-mesh gate was rattling upward. As it did, a lean dark-haired white man in black slacks and black sweater emerged from the garage, walking quickly. His hands were empty, but Brother Blood's practiced, suspicious eyes picked out the ex-con.

"That's him," he said to his driver. "Run him down."

Much too late, Runyan heard the almost silent rush of the limo coming at him. Even as he hurled himself desperately to the side, he knew he would be dead before he hit the concrete.

That was when Louise, seat-belted in and with the accelerator floored, rammed her car into the rear fender of the limo. The impact knocked its rear sideways just enough to jerk its nose aside the necessary fraction to miss Runyan as he landed, tucked, rolled, and came up running.

Not away. At. He was aware with an edge of his consciousness that Louise's car, slewed around by the impact, had spun broadside into a power pole on the other side of the still-deserted street. No fire, no explosion, and she was trying to open her sprung door: probably unhurt. She had not only saved his life; she had bought him just enough time.

Since the windshield was bulletproof glass, the bodyguard, a thickset black gorilla with wary eyes, already had his door open and his head and arm stuck out to fire at Runyan. But Runyan was high in the air; a piston-drive snap of both legs kicked the door shut again.

The bodyguard slumped down halfway out of the car, his skull creased on one side by the edge of the door, on the other by the edge of the frame. Brother Blood, halfway out of the back door, looked up into the black eye of his bodyguard's gun in Runyan's hand. He threw his arms up and wide; Brother Blood was a survivor too. Runyan gestured him away from the car and up against the wall of the building with movements of the heavy-caliber automatic.

"I won't forget this," he said in a soft, deadly voice.

"Don't," said Runyan as if he didn't care one way or the other. He swung the gun toward the chauffeur, who was trying to fit himself under the dash like a stereo.

"I . . . I just drive, sir," the chauffeur said quickly.

Runyan gestured again. "Not anymore. Not tonight."

The chauffeur opened the door on his side and scuttled out on his hands and knees, then came erect and backed away into the center of the street, arms high, face gleaming with an earnest sweat of nonviolent intentions.

Louise had managed to kick open her car door. She ran across the street to the limo and slid in under the steering wheel. Runyan heaved the unconscious bodyguard out of the way so he could get in beside her.

"I think we probably could leave," he said mildly.

A Reason to Die

MICHAEL COLLINS

Michael Collins's first Dan Fortune novel, Act of Fear, *won the Edgar Allan Poe Award from the Mystery Writers of America for the best first mystery novel of 1967. In the eleven Dan Fortune novels since, Collins has developed his one-armed private detective into a highly original series character who tests the limits of genre fiction. "Over the last years my genre and mainstream work has been growing together rather rapidly," Collins writes. "This story, some years in the writing, is another jump in that direction."*

Michael Collins is one of five pseudonyms of novelist Dennis Lynds, who presently lives in southern California. His most recent Dan Fortune novel, Harlot's Cry, *is seeking a publisher, and his Mark Sadler novel,* Deadly Innocents, *will be published early in 1986 by Walker.*

THERE ARE MANY KINDS of courage. Maybe the hardest is doing what you have to do. No matter how it looks to other people or what happens in the end.

Irish Johnny's Tavern is a gray frame house near the railroad tracks in Syracuse, New York. A beacon of red and blue neon through the mounded old snow in the dusk of another cold winter day too far from Chelsea.

My missing left arm hurt in the cold, and one of the people I was meeting was a killer.

I'd been in Irish Johnny's before, on my first day in Syracuse looking for why Alma Jean Brant was dead. Her mother had sent me.

"You go to Irish Johnny's, Mr. Fortune," Sada Patterson said. "They'll tell you about my Alma Jean."

"What can they tell me, Mrs. Patterson?" I said. I'd read the Syracuse Police Department's report, made my voice as gentle as I could in the winter light of my office-apartment loft above Eighth Avenue.

"They can tell you my girl wasn't walkin' streets without she got a reason, and whatever that there reason was it got to be what killed her."

"Every girl on the streets has a reason, Mrs. Patterson," I said.

"I don't mean no reason everyone got. I means a special reason. Somethin' made her do what she never would do," Sada Patterson said.

"Mrs. Patterson, listen—"

"No! You listen here to me." She held her old black plastic handbag in both hands on the lap of her starched print dress and fixed me across the desk with unflinching eyes. "I did my time hookin' when I was a girl. My man he couldn't get no work, so one day he ain't there no more, and I got two kids, and I hooked. A man got no work, he goes. A woman got no man, she hooks. But a woman got a man at home, she don't go on no streets. Not a good woman like my Alma Jean. She been married to that Indian ten years,

65

and she don't turn no tricks 'less she got a powerful reason."

"What do you want me to do, Mrs. Patterson?"

Ramrod straight, as thin and rock hard as any Yankee farmer, Sada Patterson studied me with her black eyes as if she could see every thought I'd ever had. She probably could. The ravages of sixty years of North Carolina dirt farms, the Syracuse ghetto, and New York sweatshops had left her nothing but bones and tendon, the flesh fossilized over the endless years.

"You go on up there 'n' find out who killed my Alma Jean. I can pay. I got the money. You go to Irish Johnny's and ask 'bout my Alma Jean. She ain't been inside the place in ten years, or any place like it. You tell 'em Sada sent you and they talk to you even if you is a honkie."

"It's a police job, Mrs. Patterson. Save your money."

"No cop's gonna worry hard 'bout the killin' of no black hooker. You go up there, Fortune. You find out." She stood up, the worn plastic handbag in both hands out in front of her like a shield. A grandmother in a print dress. Until you looked at her eyes. "She was my last—Alma Jean. She come when we had some money, lived in a house up there. She almos' got to finish grade school. I always dressed her so good. Like a real doll, you know? A little doll."

Inside, Irish Johnny's is a single large room with a bandstand at the far end. The bar is along the left wall, backed by bottles and fronted by red plastic stools. Tables fill the room around a small dance floor.

66

Behind the bar and the rows of bottles is a long mirror. The rear wall over the bandstand is bare, except when it is hung with a banner proclaiming the band or *artiste* to perform that night.

On the remaining two walls there is a large mural in the manner of Orozco or maybe Rivera. Full of violent, struggling ghetto figures, it was painted long ago by some forgotten radical student from the university on the hill above the tavern.

The crowd had not yet arrived, only a few tables occupied as I came in. The professor and his wife sat at a table close to the dance floor. I crossed the empty room under the lost eyes of the red, blue, and yellow people in the mural.

I knew who the killer was, but I didn't know how I was going to prove it. Someone was going to have to help me before I made the call to the police.

The police are always the first stop in a new town. Lieutenant Derrida of the Syracuse Police Department was an older man. He remembered Sada Patterson.

"Best-looking hooker ever walked a street in Syracuse." His thin eyes were bright and sad at the same time, as if he wished he and Sada Patterson could be back there when she had been the best-looking hooker in Syracuse, but knew it was too late for both of them.

"What made Alma Jean go to the streets, Lieutenant?"

He shrugged. "What makes any of 'em?"

"What does?" I said.

"Don't shit me, Fortune. A new car or a fur coat.

Suburbs to Saskatchewan. It just happens more in the slums where the bucks ain't so big or easy."

"Sada says no way unless the girl had a large reason," I said. "She didn't mean a fur coat or a watch."

"Sada Patterson's a mother," Derrida said.

"She's also a client. Can I earn my fee?"

He opened a desk drawer, took out a skinny file. "Alma Jean was found a week ago below a street bridge over the tracks. Some kids going to school spotted her. The fall killed her. She died somewhere between midnight and four A.M., the snow and cold made it hard to be sure. It stopped snowing about two A.M., there was no snow on top of her, so she died after that."

Derrida swiveled in his chair, looked out his single window at the gray sky and grayer city. "She could have fallen, jumped, or been pushed. There was no sign of a struggle, but she was a small woman; one push would have knocked her over that low parapet. M.E. says a bruise on her jaw could have come from a blow or from hitting a rock. No suicide note, but the snow showed someone had climbed up on the parapet. Only whoever it was didn't get near the edge, held to a light pole, jumped off the other way back onto the street."

"What's her pimp say?"

"Looks like she was trying to work independent."

I must have stared. Derrida nodded.

"I know," he said, "we sweated the pimp in the neighborhood. Black as my captain, but tells everyone he's a Polack. He says he didn't even know Alma Jean, and we can't prove he did or place him around her."

"Who do you place around her?"

"That night, no one. She was out in the snow all by herself. No one saw her, heard her, or smelled her. If she turned any tricks that night, she used doorways; no johns are talking. No cash in her handbag. A bad night."

"What about other nights?"

"The husband, Joey Brant. He's a Mohawk, works high steel like most Indians. They married ten years ago, no kids and lived good. High steel pays. With her hooking he was *numero uno* suspect, only he was drinking in Cherry Valley Tavern from nine till closing with fifty witnesses. Later, the bartender, him, and ten others sobered up in a sweat lodge until dawn."

"Anyone else?"

"*Mister* Walter Ellis. Owns the numbers, runs a big book. He was an old boyfriend of Sada's, seems to have had eyes for the daughter. She was seen visiting him a couple of times recently. Just friendly calls, he says, but he got no alibi."

"That's it?"

Derrida swiveled. "No, we got a college professor named Margon and his wife. Margon was doing 'research' with Alma Jean. Maybe the wrong kind of research. Maybe the wife got mad."

I took a chair at the table with the Margons. In Irish Johnny's anyone who opened a book in the university above the ghetto was a "professor." Fred Margon was a thin, dark-haired young man in his midtwenties. His wife, Dorothy, was a beauty-contest blonde with restless eyes.

"A temple," Fred Margon said as I sat down. "The bartenders are the priests, that mural is the holy icon painted by a wandering disciple, the liquor is God."

"I think I'll scream," Dorothy Margon said. "Or is that too undignified for the wife of a scholar, a pure artist?"

Fred Margon drank his beer, looked unhappy.

"Booze is their god," Dorothy Margon said. "That's very good. Isn't that good, Mr. Fortune? You really are bright, Fred. I wonder what you ever saw in me? Just the bod, right? You like female bods at least. You like them a lot when you've got time."

"You want to leave?" Fred said.

"No, tell us why drink is their god. Go on, tell us."

"No other god ever helped them."

"Clever," Dorothy said. "Isn't he clever, Mr. Fortune? Going to do great scholarly research, teach three classes, and finish his novel all at the same time. Then there's the female bods. When he has time. Or maybe he makes time for that."

"We'll leave," Fred said.

"All day every day: scholar, teacher, novelist. For twenty whole thousand dollars a year!"

"We manage," Fred Margon said.

"Never mind," Dorothy said. "Just never mind."

I met him in a coffee shop on South Crouse after a class. He looked tired. We had coffee, and he told me about Alma Jean.

"I found her in an Indian bar six months ago. I like to walk through the city, meet the real people." He drank his coffee. "She had a way of speaking full of metaphors. I wrote my doctoral dissertation on the poetry of totally untrained people, got a grant to continue the research. I met her as often as I could. In the bars and in her home. To listen and record her speech. She was highly intelligent. Her insights were remarkable for someone without an education, and her way of expressing her thoughts was pure uneducated poetry."

"You liked her?"

He nodded. "She was real, alive."

"How much did you like her, professor?"

"Make it Fred, okay? I'm only a bottom-step assistant professor, and sometimes I want to drop the whole thing, live a real life, make some money." He drank his coffee, looked out the cafe window. He knew what I was asking. "My wife isn't happy, Mr. Fortune. When she's unhappy, she has the classic female method of showing it. Perhaps in time I would have tried with Alma Jean, but I didn't. She really wasn't interested, you know? In me or any other man. Only her husband."

"You know her husband?"

"I've met him. Mostly at her house, sometimes in a bar. He seems to drink a lot. I asked her about that. She said it was part of being an Indian, a 'brave.' Work hard and drink hard. He always seemed angry. At her, at his bosses, at everything. He didn't like me, or my being there, as if it were an insult to him, but he just sat in the living room, drinking and looking out a window at the tall buildings downtown. Sometimes he talked about working on those buildings. He was proud of that. Alma Jean said that was the culture; a 'man' did brave work, daring."

"When was the last time you saw her?"

"The day she died." He shrugged as he drank his coffee. "The police know. I had a session with her early in the day at her house. Her husband wasn't there, and she seemed tired, worried. She'd been unhappy for months, I think, but it was always hard to tell with her. Always cheerful and determined. I told her there was a book in her life, but she only scorned the idea. Life was to be lived, not written about. When there were troubles, you did something."

"What troubles sent her out on the streets?"

He shook his head. "She never told me. A few weeks ago she asked me to pay her for making the tapes. She needed money. I couldn't pay her much on my grant, but I gave her what I could. I know it wasn't anywhere near enough. I heard her talking on the telephone, asking about the cost of something."

"You don't know what?"

"No." He drank coffee. "But whoever she was talking to offered to pay for whatever it was. She turned him down."

"You're sure it was a him?"

"No, I'm not sure."

"Who killed her, professor?"

Outside, the students crunched through the snow

in the gray light. He watched them as if he wished he were still one of them, his future unknown. "I don't know who killed her, Mr. Fortune. I know she didn't commit suicide, and I doubt that she fell off that bridge. I never saw her drunk. When her husband drank, she never did, as if she had to be sober to take care of him."

"Where were you that night?"

"At home," he said, looked up at me. "But I couldn't sleep, another argument with my wife. So I went out walking in the snow. Didn't get back until two A.M. or so."

"Was it still snowing?"

"It had just stopped when I got home."

"Did you see anyone while you were out?"

"Not Alma Jean, if that's what you want to know. I did see that older friend of hers. What's his name? Walter Ellis?"

"Where?"

"Just driving around. That pink Caddy of his is easy to remember. Especially in the snow, so few cars driving."

"And all you were doing with her was recording her speech?"

He finished his coffee. "That's all, Mr. Fortune."

After he left, I paid for the coffee. He was an unhappy man, and not just about money or work.

The scar-faced man stood just inside the door. Snow dripped from his dirty raincoat into a pool around his black boots. A broad, powerfully built man with a fresh bandage on his face. Dark stains covered the front of his raincoat. The raincoat and his black shirt were open at the throat. He wore a large silver cross bedded in the hair of his chest.

"Now there's something you can write about," Dorothy Margon said. "Real local color. Who is he? What is he? Why don't you make notes. You didn't forget your notebook, did you, Fred?"

"His name is Duke," Fred Margon said. "He's a pimp, and this is his territory. A small-time pimp, only three girls on the street now. He takes 80 percent of what they make to protect them, lets them support him with most of the rest. But the competition is fierce, and business is bad this season. He gives students a cut rate; professors pay full price."

"Of course," Dorothy said. "Part of your 'research' into 'ordinary' people. All for art and scholarship." She looked at the man at the entrance. "I wonder what his girls are like. Are they young or old? Do they admire him? I suppose they all love him. Of course they do. All three of them in love with him."

"In love with him and afraid of him," I said.

"Love and fear," Fred Margon said. "Their world."

"Do I hear a story?" Dorothy said. "Is everything a story? Nothing real? With results? Change? A future?"

I watched him come across the dance floor toward our table. Duke Wiltkowski, the pimp in the streets where Alma Jean had been found dead.

· · ·

The pimp's office was a cellar room with a single bare bulb, a table for a desk, some battered armchairs, a kerosene heater, and water from melted snow pooled in a dark corner. Times had been better for Duke Wiltkowski.

"You sayin' I killed her? You sayin' that, man?" His black face almost hidden in the shadows of the cellar room, the light of the bare bulb barely reaching where he sat behind the table.

"Someone did," I said. "You had a motive."

"You say I kill that chippie, you got trouble, man. I got me a good lawyer. He sue you for everythin' you got!"

"The police say she was in your territory."

"The police is lyin'! The police say I kill that chippie, they lyin'!" His voice was high and thin, almost hysterical. It's a narrow world of fear, his world. On the edge. Death on one side, prison on the other, hunger and pain in between.

"She was free-lance in your territory. You can't let her do that. Not and survive. Let her do that, and you're out of business."

He sat in the gloom of the cold basement room, unmoving in the half shadows. The sweat shone on his face like polished ebony. The face of a rat with his back to the wall, cornered. Protesting.

"I never see that chippie. Not me. How I know she was working my turf? You tell the cops that, okay? You tell the cops Duke Wiltkowski never nowhere near that chippie."

He sweated in the cold cellar room. A depth in his

wide eyes almost of pleading. Go away, leave him alone. Go away before he told what he couldn't tell. Wanted to tell but couldn't. Not yet.

"Where were you that night?"

"Right here. An' with one o' my pigs. All night. Milly-O. Me 'n' Milly-O we was makin' it most all night. You asks her."

One of his prostitutes who would say anything he told her to say, to the police or to God himself. That desperate. An alibi he knew was no alibi. Sweated. Licked his lips.

"That Injun husband she got, maybe he done it. Hey, they all crazy, them Injuns! That there professor hangs in Irish Johnny's. Hey, he got to of been playin' pussy with her. I mean, a big-shot white guy down there. Hey, that there professor he got a wife. Maybe she don't like that chippie, right?"

"How about Walter Ellis? He was out in the snow that night."

The fear on his face became sheer terror. "I don' know nothin' 'bout Mr. Ellis! You hears, Fortune! Nothin'!"

Now he walked into Irish Johnny's with the exaggerated swing and lightness of a dancer. Out in public, the big man. His face in the light a mass of crisscross scars. The new bandage dark with dried blood. He smiled a mouthful of broken yellow teeth.

"Saw it was you, professor. That your lady?" He clicked his heels, bowed to Dorothy Margon. A Prussian officer. "Duke Wiltkowski. My old man was

Polack." He nodded to me, cool and casual, expansive. An image to keep up and no immediate fear in sight. "Hey, Fortune. How's the snoopin'?"

"Slow," I said, smiled. "But getting there."

"Yeh." The quick lick of the lips, and sat down at the table, legs out in his Prussian boots. The silver cross at his throat reflected the bright tavern light. He surveyed the room with a cool, imperious eye. Looked at Dorothy Margon. "You been holdin' out on the Duke, professor. You could do real business with that one."

The Duke admired Dorothy's long blonde hair, the low-cut black velvet dress that looked too expensive for an assistant professor's wife, her breasts rising out of the velvet.

"It's not what I do," Fred Margon said.

Dorothy Margon tore a cardboard coaster into small pieces, dropped the pieces onto the table. She began to build the debris into a pyramid. She worked on her pyramid, watched the Duke.

The people were filling the tavern now. I watched them come out of the silence and cold of the winter night into the light and noise of the tavern. They shed old coats and worn jackets, wool hats and muddy galoshes, to emerge in suits and dresses the colors of the rainbow. Saturday night.

The Duke sneered. "Works their asses a whole motherin' year for the rags they got on their backs." He waved imperiously to a waiter. "Set 'em up for my man the professor 'n' his frau. Fortune there too. Rye for me."

Dorothy Margon built her pyramid of torn pieces of coaster. "What happened to your face?"

"Injuns." The Duke touched the bandage on his face, his eyes fierce. "The fuckers ganged me. I get 'em."

"Alma Jean's husband?" I said. "The Cherry Valley bar?"

The Cherry Valley Tavern was a low-ceilinged room with posts and tables and a long bar with high stools. As full of dark Iroquois faces as the massacre that had given it its name. All turned to look at me as I entered. I ordered a beer.

The bartender brought me the beer. "Maybe you'd like it better downtown, mister. Nothing personal."

"I'm looking for Joey Brant."

He mopped the bar. "You're not a cop."

"Private. Hired by his mother-in-law."

He went on mopping the bar.

"She wants to know who killed her daughter."

"Brant was in here all night."

"They told me. What time do you close?"

"Two."

"When the snow stopped," I said.

"We went to the sweat lodge. Brant too."

"Good way to sober up on a cold night. Maybe Brant has some ideas about who did kill her."

"Down the end of the bar."

He was a small man alone on the last bar stool. He sat hunched, a glass in both hands. An empty glass. Brooding into the glass or staring up at himself in the bar mirror. I stood behind him. He didn't notice, waved at the bartender, violent and arrogant.

"You had enough, Joey."

"I says when I got enough." He scowled at the bartender. The bartender did nothing. Brant looked down at his empty glass. "I got no woman, Crow. She's dead, Crow. My woman. How I'm gonna live my woman's dead?"

"You get another woman," the bartender, Crow, said.

Brant stared at his empty glass, remembered what he wanted. "C'mon, Crow."

"You ain't got two paychecks now."

Brant swung his head from side to side as if caught in the mesh of a net, thrashing in the net. "Lemme see the stuff."

The bartender opened a drawer behind the bar, took out a napkin, opened it on the bar. Various pieces of silver and turquoise Indian jewelry lay on the towel. There were small red circles of paper attached to most pieces. Rings, bracelets, pendants, pins, a silver cross. Joey Brant picked up a narrow turquoise ring. It was one of the last pieces without a red tag.

"Two bottles," Crow said.

"It's real stuff, Crow. Four?"

"Two."

I thought Brant was going to cry, but he only nodded. Crow took an unopened bottle of cheap rye blend from under the bar, wrote on it. Close, Brant's shoulders were thickly muscled, his arms powerful, his neck like a bull. A flyweight bodybuilder. Aware of his body, his image. I sat on the stool beside him. He stared at my empty sleeve. Crow put a shot glass and a small beer on the bar, opened the marked bottle of rye.

"On me," I said. "Both of us."

Crow stared at me, then closed the marked bottle, poured from a bar bottle. He brought my beer and a chaser beer, walked away. The small, muscular Indian looked at the whisky, at me.

"Why was Alma Jean on the street, Joey?" I said.

He looked down at the whisky. His hand seemed to wait an inch from the shot glass. Then he touched it, moved it next to the beer chaser.

"How the hell I know? The bitch."

"Her mother says she had to have a big reason."

"Fuck her mother." He glared at my missing arm. "You no cop. Cops don't hire no cripples."

"Dan Fortune. Private detective. Sada Patterson hired me to find out who murdered Alma Jean. Any ideas?"

He stared into the shot glass of cheap rye as if it held all the beauty of the universe. "She think I don' know? Stupid bitch an' her black whoremaster! I knows he give her stuff. I get him, you watch. Make him talk. Black bastard, he done it sure. I get him." He drank, went on staring into the bottom of the glass as if it were a crystal ball. "Fuckin' around with that white damn professor. Think she fool Joey Brant? Him an' that hot-bitch wife he got. Business, she says; old friends, she says. Joey knows, yessir. Joey knows."

"You knew," I said, "so you killed her."

There was a low rumble through the room. The bartender, Crow, stopped pouring to watch me. They didn't love Brant, but he was one of them, and they would defend him against the white man. Any white man, black or white.

Brant shook his head. "With my friends. Not worth killin'. Nossir. Joey Brant takes care of hisself." He drained the shot, finished the beer chaser, and laid his head on the bar.

The bartender came and removed the glasses, watched me finish my beer. When I did, he made no move to serve another.

"He was in here all night; fifty guys saw him. We went to the reservation and sweated. Me and ten other guys and Brant."

"Sure," I said.

I felt their eyes all the way out. They didn't like him, even despised him, but they would all defend him, lie for him.

The band burst into sound. Dancers packed into a mass on the floor. A thick mass of bodies that moved as one, the colors and shapes of the mural on the wall, a single beast with a hundred legs and arms. Shrill tenor sax, electronic guitar, keyboard, and trumpet blaring. Drums.

"Or did Brant find you?" I said.

The Duke scowled at the dancers on the floor. "Heard he was lookin' to talk to the Duke, so I goes to the Cherry Valley. He all shit and bad booze. He never know me, 'n' I never knows him. I tells him I hear he talkin' 'bout me 'n' from now on all I wants to hear is sweet nothin'.'"

"You're a tough man," I said. "I'll bet you scared him."

He licked his lips. I watched the sweat on his brow, the violent swinging of his booted foot. He was hiding *something*.

"I tell him I never even heard o' his broad. What I know about no Injun's broad? I tell him iffen she goes out on the tricks, it got to be he put her out. Happens all the time. Some ol' man he needs the scratch, so he puts the ol' woman out on the hustle." The swinging foot in its black boot seemed to grow more agitated. His eyes searched restlessly around the packed room, the crowded dance floor. "I seen it all times, all ways. They comes out on the streets, nice chicks should oughta be home watchin' the kids, puttin' the groceries on the table. I seen 'em, scared 'n' no way knows what they s'posed to do. All 'cause some dude he ain't got what it takes."

Restless, he sweated. The silver cross reflected the tavern light where it lay on his thick chest hair above the black shirt. Talked. But what was he telling me?

"Is that when he jumped you? Pulled a knife?"

The Duke sneered. "Not him. He too drunk. All of 'em, they ganged me. He pull his blade, sure, but he ain't sober 'nuff he can cut cheese. It was them others ganged me. I got some of 'em, got out o' there."

"Did you see him out on the street that night, Duke? Is that what you really told him? Why they ganged on you?"

He jerked back as if snakebitten. "I ain't seen no one that there night! I ain't on the street that there night. I—"

He stared toward the door. As if he saw a demon.

Joey Brant stood inside the tavern entrance blinking at the noise and crowd. Walter Ellis stood beside Brant. Which one was the Duke's demon?

It was a big house by Syracuse-ghetto standards. A two-story, three-bedroom, cinder-block box painted yellow and green, with a spiked wrought-iron fence, a swimming pool that took up most of the postage-stamp side yard. Concrete paths wound among birdbaths and fountains and the American flag on a pole and naked plaster copies of the Venus de Milo and Michelangelo's David.

Walter Ellis met me on his front steps. "The cops send you to me, Fortune?"

He was a tall, slim man with snow-white hair and a young face. He looked dangerous. Quick eyes that smiled now. Simple gray flannel slacks, a white shirt open at the throat, and a red cashmere sweater that gave a vigorous tint to his face. Only the rings on both pinkies and both index fingers, diamonds and rubies and gold, showed his money and his power.

"They said you knew Alma Jean Brant," I said.

"Her and her mother. Come on in. Drink?"

"Beer if you have it."

He laughed. "Now you know I got beer. What kind of rackets boss wouldn't have a extra refrigerator full of beer? Beck's? Stroh's? Bud?"

"Beck's, thanks."

"Sure. A New York loner."

We were in a small, cluttered, overstuffed living room all lace and velvet and cushions. Ellis pressed a button somewhere. A tall, handsome black man in full suit and tie materialized, not the hint of a bulge anywhere under the suit, was told to bring two Beck's.

"Not that I'm much of a racket boss like in the movies, eh? A small-town gambler. Maybe a little border stuff if the price is right." He laughed again, sat down in what had to be his private easy chair, worn and comfortable with a footstool, waved me to an overstuffed couch. I sank into it. He lit a cigar, eyed me over it. "But you didn't come about my business, right? Sada sent you up to find out what happened to Alma Jean."

"What did happen to her?"

"I wish I knew."

The immaculate black returned with two Beck's and two glasses on an ornate silver tray. A silver bowl of bar peanuts. Ellis raised his glass. We drank. He ate peanuts and smoked.

"You liked her?" I said. "Alma Jean?"

He savored the cigar. "I liked her. She was married. That's all. Not my age or anything else. She didn't cheat on her husband. A wife supports her husband."

"But she went on the streets."

"Prostitution isn't cheating, Fortune. Not in the ghetto, not down here where it hurts. It's the only way a woman has of making money when she got no education or skills. It's what our women do to help in a crisis."

"And the men accept that?"

He smoked, drank, fingered peanuts. "Some do, some don't."

"Which are you?"

"I never cottoned to white slaving."

"You were out that night. In your car. On the streets down near Irish Johnny's.

He drank, licked foam from his lips. "Who says?"

"Professor Fred Margon saw you. I think Duke Wiltkowski did too. He's scared, sweating, and hiding something."

His eyes were steady over the glass, the peanuts he ate one by one. "I like a drive, a nice walk in the snow. I saw the Duke and Margon. I didn't see no one else. But a couple of times I saw that wife of Margon's tailing Alma Jean."

"Was it snowing when you got home?"

He smiled.

I watched Walter Ellis steer Joey Brant to a table on the far side of the dance floor. Brant was already drunk, but his startled eyes were wary, almost alert. This wasn't one of his taverns. The Duke watched Walter Ellis.

I said, "It's okay; we know he was out that night. He saw you, knows you saw him, and it's okay. Who else did you see?"

The Duke licked his lips, looked at Fred Margon.

"You writes, yeh, professor?"

He looked back across the dance floor to Ellis and Joey Brant.

"I means," the Duke said, "like stories 'n' books 'n' all that there?"

"God, does he write!" Dorothy Margon said. "Writes, studies, teaches. All day, every day. Tell the Duke about your art, Fred. Tell the Duke what you *do*. All day, every damn day."

"Like," the Duke said, "poetry stuff?" He watched only Fred Margon now. "Words they got the same sound 'n' all?"

"I write poetry," Fred said. "Sometimes it rhymes."

"You likes poetry, yeh?"

"Yes, I like poetry. I read it."

"Oh, but it's so hard!" Dorothy said. "Tell the Duke how hard poetry is, Fred. Tell him how hard all *real* writing is. Tell him how you can learn most careers in a few years but it takes a lifetime to learn to write well."

"We better go," Fred said.

I watched the people packed body to body on the dance floor, flushed and excited, desperate for Saturday night. On the far side Walter Ellis ordered drinks. Joey Brant saw us: the Duke, me, Fred and Dorothy Margon. I watched him turn on Ellis. The racket boss only smiled, shook his head.

Dorothy smiled at the Duke. "I'm a bitch, right? I wasn't once. Do your women talk to you like that, Duke? No, they wouldn't, would they? They wouldn't dare. They wouldn't want to. Tell me about the Indians? How many were there? Did they all have knives? Do they still wear feathers? How many did you knock out? Kill?"

The Duke watched Fred Margon. "You writes good, professor?"

"You see," Dorothy said, "we're going to stay at the university three more years. We may even stay forever. Isn't that grand news? I can stay here and do nothing forever."

The Duke said to Fred, "They puts what you writes in books?"

Dorothy said, "Did you ever want something, wait for something, think you have it at last, and then suddenly it's so far away again you can't even see it anymore?"

"I'm a writer," Fred said. "A writer and a teacher. I can't go to New York and write lies for money."

Dorothy stood up. "Dance with me, Duke. I want to dance. I want to dance right now."

She opened the apartment door my second day in Syracuse, looked at my duffel coat, beret, and missing arm.

"He's out. Go find him in one of your literary bars!"

"Mrs. Margon?" I said.

She cocked her head, suspicious yet coy, blonde and flirtatious. "You want me?"

"Would it do me any good?"

She laughed. "Do we know each other, Mr.—?"

"Fortune," I said. "No."

She eyed me. "Then what do you want to talk to me about?"

"Alma Jean Brant," I said.

She started to close the door. "Go and find my husband."

I held the door with my foot. "No, I want you. Both ways."

She laughed again, neither flirtatious nor amused this time. Self-mocking, a little bitter. "You can probably have me. Both ways." But stepped back, held the door open. "Come in."

It was a small apartment: a main room, bedroom, kitchenette, and bathroom. All small, cramped. The furniture had to have been rented with the apartment. They don't pay assistant professors too well, and the future of a writer is at best a gamble, so without children they saved their money, scrimped, did without. She lit a cigarette, didn't offer me one.

"What about that Alma Jean woman?"

"What can you tell me about her?"

"Nothing. That's Fred's territory. Ask him."

"About her murder?"

She smoked. "I thought it was an accident. Or suicide. Drunk and fell over that bridge wall, or jumped. Isn't that what the police think?"

"The police don't think anything one way or the other. I think it was murder."

"What do you want, Mr. Fortune? A confession?"

"Do you want to make one?"

"Yes, that I'm a nasty bitch who wants more than she's got. Just more. You understand that, Mr. Fortune."

"It's a modern disease," I said, "but what's it got to do with Alma Jean Brant?"

She smoked. "You wouldn't be here if someone hadn't seen me around her."

"Her husband," I said. "And Walter Ellis."

The couch creaked under her as if it had rusty springs. "I was jealous. Or maybe just suspicious. He's so involved in his work, I'm so bored, our sex life is about zero. We never do anything! We talk, read, think, discuss, but we never *do*! I make his life miserable, I admit it. But he promised we would stay here only five years or until he published a novel. We would go down to New York, he'd make money, we'd have some life! I counted on that. Now he wants to get tenure, stay here!"

"So he can teach and write?" I said. "That's all? No other reason for wanting to stay here?"

She nodded. "When he started going out all the time, I wondered too. Research for his work, he said, but I heard about Alma Jean. So I followed him and found where she lived. Then I followed her to see if she'd meet him somewhere else. That's all. I just watched her house, followed her a few times. I never saw him do a damn thing that could be close to cheating. At her house that husband of hers was around all the time. He must work nights."

"Did you see her do anything?"

She smoked. "I saw her visit the same house three or four times. I got real suspicious then. I hadn't seen Fred go in, but after she left the last time, I went up and rang the bell. A guy answered, but it wasn't Fred, so I made some excuse and got out of there. She was meeting someone all right, but not Fred."

"Any idea who?"

She shook her head. "He wasn't an Indian, I can say that."

"What was he?"

"Black, Mr. Fortune. One big black man."

Through the mass of sound and movement, bodies and faces that glistened with sweat and gaudy color and melted into the bright colors and tortured figures of the mural on the walls, I watched Joey Brant across the dance floor drinking and talking to Walter Ellis, who only listened.

I watched Dorothy Margon move lightly through the shuffle of the massed dancers. Her slender body loose and supple, her eyes closed, her lips parted, her face turned up to the Duke. I could see a man she denied turn to someone else. A man who could not give her what she wanted turning to someone who wanted less.

Her hips moved a beat behind the band; her long blonde hair swung free against the black velvet of her dress and the scarred face of the Duke. I could see her, restless and rejecting, but still not wanting her man to go anywhere else.

"I can't tell the dancers from the people in the mural," Fred Margon said. "I can't be sure which woman is my wife with the Duke and which is the woman chained in the mural."

He was talking about himself: a man who could not tell which was real and which was only an image. He could not decide, be certain, which was real to him, image or reality.

"Which man is the Duke on the dance floor with my wife," Fred Margon said, "and which is the blue man with the bare chest and hammer in the mural? Am I the man at the ringside table with a glass of beer in a pale, indoor hand watching the Duke dance with his wife, or the thin scarecrow in the mural with his wrists chained and his starving face turned up to an empty sky?"

He was trying to understand something, and across the dance floor Joey Brant was talking and talking to Walter Ellis. Ellis only listened and watched the Duke and Dorothy Margon on the dance floor. The Duke sweated, and Dorothy Margon danced with her eyes closed, her body moving as if by itself.

Walter Ellis sat alone in the back of his pink Cadillac. I leaned in the window.

"A black man, she said. A big black man Alma Jean visited in a house in the ghetto."

"A lot of big black men in the ghetto, Fortune."

"What was the crisis?" I said. "You said going on the streets was what ghetto women did in a crisis."

91

"I don't know."

"You offered to pay for whatever she needed money for."

"She only told me she needed something that cost a lot of money."

"Needed what?"

"A psychiatrist. I sent her to the best."

"A black? Big? Lives near here? Expensive?"

"All that."

"Can we go and talk to him?"

"Anytime."

"And you didn't give her the money to pay him?"

"She wouldn't take it. Said she would know what it was really for even if it was only in my mind."

The Duke said, "There was this here chippie. I mean, she's workin' my streets 'n' I don' work her, see? I mean, it's snowin' bad 'n' there ain't no action goin' down, my three pigs're holed up warmin' their pussy, but this chippie she's out workin' on my turf. Hey, that don't go down, you know? I mean, that's no scene, right? So I moves in to tell her to fly her pussy off'n my streets or sign up with the Duke."

I said, "The last time it snowed was the night Alma Jean died."

Dorothy Margon built another pyramid of torn coasters on the tavern table and watched the Saturday night dancers. Fred Margon and I watched the Duke. The Duke mopped his face with a dirty handkerchief, a kind of desperation in his voice that rose higher, faster, as if he could not stop himself, had to talk while Fred Margon was there.

"I *knows* that there fox. I mean, I gets up close to tell her do a fade and I remembers that chippie in the snow."

I said, "It was Alma Jean."

He sweated in that hot room with its pounding music and packed bodies swirling and rubbing. It was what he had been hiding, holding back. What he had wanted to tell from the start. What he had to tell.

"Back when I was jus' a punk kid stealin' dogs, my ol' man beatin' my ass to go to school, that there chippie out in the snow was in that school. I remembers. Smart 'n' clean 'n' got a momma dresses her up real good. I remembers, you know? Like, I had eyes for that pretty little kid back then."

The band stopped. The dancers drifted off the floor, sat down. A silence like a blow from a hammer in the hands of the big blue man in the mural.

"I walks off. I mean, when I remembers that little girl, I walks me away from that there chippie. I remembers how good her momma fixes her up, so I walks off 'n' lets her work, 'n' I got the blues, you know. I got the blues then, 'n' I got 'em now."

"Everybody got the blues," Dorothy said. "We should write a song. Fred should write a poem."

"It was Alma Jean, Duke," I said.

Walter Ellis stopped to say a few low words to the tall, handsome doctor, while I walked down the steps of his modest house and out to the ghetto street. The numbers boss caught up with me before I reached his Cadillac.

"Does that tell you who killed her?" Ellis said.

"I think so. All I have to do is find a way to prove it."

He nodded. We both got into the back of the pink car. It purred away from the curb. The silent driver in the immaculate suit drove slowly, sedately, parading Ellis through his domain where the people could see him.

"Any ideas?" Ellis said.

"Watch and hope for a break. They've all got something on their minds; maybe it'll get too heavy."

He watched the street ahead. "That include me?"

"It includes you," I said. "You were out that night."

"You know what I've got on my mind?"

"I've got a hunch," I said. "I'm going to meet the Margons in Irish Johnny's tonight. Why don't you come around and bring Brant, friend of the family."

We drove on to my motel.

"The Duke hangs out in Irish Johnny's," Ellis said.

"I know," I said.

"I writes me a poem," the Duke said. " 'Bout that there chippie. I go home 'n' writes me a poem."

The scarred black face of the Duke seemed to watch the empty dance floor as he told about the poem he had written. Fred Margon looked at him. All through the long room the Saturday night people waited for the music to begin again. Across the floor Walter Ellis talked to those who came to him one by one to pay their respects. Joey Brant drank, stared into his glass, looked toward me and the Margons and the Duke.

"Do you have it with you?" Fred said.

The Duke's eyes flickered above the scars on his face and the new bandage. Looked right and left.

"Did you bring it to show me?" Fred Margon said.

The Duke sweated in the hot room. Nodded.

"All right," Fred said. "But don't just show it to me, read it. Out loud. Poetry should be read aloud. While the band is still off, get up and read your poem. This is your tavern; they all know you in here. Tell them why you wrote it, how it came to you, and read it to them."

The Duke stared. "You fuckin' with me, man?"

"Fred?" Dorothy Margon said.

"You wrote it, didn't you? You felt it. If you feel something and write it, you have to believe in it. You have to show it to the world, make the world hear."

"You a crazy man," the Duke said.

Dorothy tore another coaster. Across the room Joey Brant and Walter Ellis watched our table. I waited.

"Give it to me," Fred said.

The Duke sat there for some time, the sweat beaded on his face, his booted foot swinging, while the people all through the room waited for Saturday night to return.

"What happened to Alma Jean, Duke?" I said.

Fred Margon said, "You wrote it; give it to me."

95

The Duke reached into his filthy raincoat and handed a torn piece of lined notebook paper to Fred Margon. Fred stood up. On the other side of the dance floor Joey Brant held his glass without drinking as Fred Margon walked to the bandstand, jumped up to the microphone.

"Ladies and gentlemen!"

In the long room, ice loud in the glasses and voices in the rumble of conversation, the people who waited only for the music to begin again, Saturday night to return, turned toward the bandstand. Fred Margon told them about the Duke and the chippie working his territory without his permission. The Duke alone in the night with the snow and the chippie.

"The Duke remembered that girl. He let her work, went home and wrote a poem. I'm going to read that poem."

There were some snickers, a murmur of protest or two, the steady clink of indifferent glasses. Fred called for silence. Waited. Until the room silenced. Then he read the poem.

> *Once I was pure*
> *as a snow but I fell,*
> *fell like a snowflake*
> *from heaven to hell.*
>
> *Fell to be scuffed,*
> *to be spit on and beat,*
> *fell to be like*
> *the filth in the street.*

Pleading and cursing
and dreading to die
to the fellow I know
up there in the sky.

The fellow his cross
I got on this chain
I give it to her
she gets clean again.

Dear God up there,
have I fell so low,
and yet to be once
like the beautiful snow.

Through the smoke haze of the crowded tavern room
they shifted their feet. They stirred their drinks. The
musicians, ready to return, stood in the wings. A
woman giggled. The bartenders hid grins. Some men
suddenly laughed. A murmur of laughter rippled
through the room. The Duke stood up, stepped toward
the bandstand. Fred came across the empty dance
floor.

"I like it," Fred Margon said. "It's not a good poem;
you're not a poet. But it's real and I like it. I like anything that says what you really feel, says it openly and
honestly. It's what you had to do."

The Duke's eyes were black above the scars and the
bandage. The Duke watched only Fred, his fists
clenched, his eyes wide.

"It's you," Fred said. "Go up and read it yourself.
Make them see what you saw out there in the snow

when you remembered Alma Jean, the girl whose mother dressed her so well. To hell with anyone who laughs. They're laughing at themselves. The way they would have laughed if Alma Jean had told them what she was going to do. They're afraid, so they laugh. They're afraid to know what they feel. They're afraid to feel. Help them face themselves. Read your poem again. And again."

The Duke stood in Irish Johnny's Tavern, five new stitches in his scarred face under the bandage, and read his poem to the people who only wanted Saturday night to start again with the loud blare of the music and the heavy mass of the dancing and a kind of oblivion. He read without stumbling over the words, not reading but hearing it in the smoke of the gaudy tavern room. Hearing it as it had come to him when he stood in the snow and remembered the girl whose mother had always dressed her so well.

There was no laughter now. The Duke was doing what he had to do. Fred and Dorothy Margon were listening, and no one wanted to look stupid. Walter Ellis and Joey Brant were listening, and no one wanted to offend Mr. Ellis. So they sat, and the band waited to come back and start Saturday night again, and I went to the telephone and called Lieutenant Derrida.

Walter Ellis moved his chair, and I faced Joey Brant across the tavern table. "High steel pays good money, but you haven't been making good money in a long time. You were home whenever Professor Margon went to talk to Alma Jean. You were home when Dorothy Margon watched Alma Jean. You haven't been working high steel for over a year. That's why she went out on the streets. You even had to sell Alma Jean's jewelry to buy whisky at Cherry Valley Tavern. One of those pieces wasn't hers, though, and that was a mistake. It was the cross the Duke gave her the night she was killed, the one he wrote about in his poem. You knew someone else had given it to her, but you didn't know the Duke had given it to her that night, and it proves you killed her. You grabbed it from her neck before you knocked her off that bridge."

Lieutenant Derrida stood over the table. The room was watching now. The Duke with his poem in his hand, Walter Ellis sad, Fred and Dorothy Margon holding hands but not looking at each other. Derrida said, "It's the cross the Duke gave her that night, has his initials inside. Your boss says you haven't worked high steel in over a year, just low-pay ground jobs when you show up at all. When the bartender, Crow, saw we had proof and motive, he talked. You left the tavern when it closed, didn't get to the sweat lodge until pushing 3:30 A.M. You brought the jewelry to Crow after she was dead."

Joey Brant drained his whisky, looked at us all with rage in his dark eyes. "She didn't got to go on no streets. We was makin' it all right. She got no cause playin' with white guys, sellin' it to old men, working for black whoremasters. I cut him good, that black bastard, 'n' I knocked her off that there bridge when she was out selling her ass so she could live high and

99

rich with her white friends and her gamblers and her black pimps! Sure, I hit her. I never meant to kill her, but I saw that cross on her neck 'n' I never give her no cross 'n' I hit her and she went on over."

I said, "Her mother said she would only go on the streets for a big reason. You know what that was, Brant? You know why she went back on the streets?"

"I know, mister. Money, that's why! 'Cause I ain't bringing home the big bucks like the gambler 'n' the professor 'n' the black pimp!"

"She wanted to hire a psychiatrist," I said. "You know what that is, Joey. A man who makes a sick mind get better."

"Psychiatrist?" Joey Brant said.

"A healer, Joey. For a scared man who sat at home all day and drank too much. An expensive healer, so she had to go out on the streets to make the money she couldn't make any other way."

"Shut up, you hear? Shut up!" His dark face almost white.

I shook my head. "We know, Joey. We talked to the psychiatrist and your boss. You're afraid of heights, Joey. You couldn't even go to the edge of that bridge parapet and see where she had fallen. You can't go up high on the steel anymore, where the big money is. Where a brave goes. Up there with the real men. You became afraid and it was killing you and that was killing her and she had to try to help you, save you, so she wanted money to take you to a psychiatrist who would cure you, help you go up on the steel again where you could feel like a man!"

"Psychiatrist?" Joey Brant said.

"That's right, Joey. Her big, special reason to make big money the only way she knew how."

Joey Brant sat there for a long time looking at all of us, at the floor, at his hands, at his empty whisky glass. Just sat while Lieutenant Derrida waited and everyone drifted away, and at last he put his head down on the table and began to cry.

Derrida had taken Joey Brant away. The Duke had stopped reading his poem to anyone who would listen. I sat at the floor-side table with Fred and Dorothy Margon. Out on the floor the Saturday night people clung and twined and held each other in their fine shimmering clothes, while in the mural the silent yellow women and bent blue men frozen in the red and yellow sky watched and waited.

"Dance with me, Fred," Dorothy Margon said.

"I'm a bad dancer," Fred Margon said. "I always have been a bad dancer. I always will be a bad dancer."

"I know," Dorothy said. "Just dance with me now."

They danced among the faceless crowd, two more bodies that would soon go their separate ways. I knew that and so did they. Fred would teach and write and go on examining life for what he must write about. Dorothy would go to New York or Los Angeles to find more out of life than an assistant professor, a would-be writer. What they had to do.

The Duke has one kind of courage and Fred Margon has another. Joey Brant lost his. Fred Margon's kind will cost him his wife. Alma Jean's courage killed her.

The courage to do what she had to do to help her man, even though she knew he would not understand. He would hate her, but she had to do it anyway. Courage has its risks, and we don't always win.

In my New York office-apartment Sada Patterson listened in silence, her worn plastic handbag on her skinny lap, the ramrod back so straight it barely touched my chair.

"I knew she had a big reason," she said. "That was my Alma Jean. To help her man find hisself again." She nodded, almost satisfied, "I'm sorry for him. He's a little man." She stood up. "I gonna miss her—Alma Jean. She was my last: I always dressed her real good."

She paid me. I took the money. She had her courage too. And her pride. She'd go on living, fierce and independent, even if she couldn't really tell herself why.

The Ripoff: Part II

JIM THOMPSON

Jim Thompson's admirers tout his twenty-nine novels, published in paperback between 1942 and 1973, as unequaled in postwar American fiction. His work has become popular among French cinéma noir directors fascinated by existential American violence. The Ripoff, a work in progress at the time of Thompson's death, is published in NBMQ for the first time. This installment is the second of four.

The story thus far: Britton Rainstar, the impecunious son of a disgraced American Indian professor, lives in the run-down mansion that formerly belonged to his family, on the edge of an encroaching garbage dump. He is recruited to write for the PXA Holding Company by Manuela Aloe, who becomes his lover. Then inexplicable—and frightening—things begin to happen.

8

MORE THAN A MONTH went by before I met Patrick Xavier Aloe. It was at a party at his house, and Manny and I went to it together.

Judging by his voice, the one telephone conversation I had had with him, I supposed him to be a towering giant of a man. But while he was broad-shouldered and powerful looking, he was little taller than Manny.

"Glad to finally meet up with you, Britt, baby." He

beamed at me out of his broad, darkly Irish face. "What have you got under your arm there? One of Manny's pizzas?"

"He has the complete manuscript of a pamphlet," Manny said proudly. "And it's darned good, too!"

"It is, huh? What d'ya say, Britt? Is she telling the truth or not?"

"Well . . ." I hesitated modestly. "I'm sure there's room for improvement, but—"

"We'll see, we'll see," he broke in, laughing. "You two grab a drink and come on."

We followed him through the small crowd of guests, all polite and respectable-appearing, but perhaps a little on the watchful side. We went into the library, and Pat Aloe waved us to chairs, then sat down behind the desk, carefully removed my manuscript from its envelope, and began to read.

He read rapidly but intently, with no skimming or skipping. I could tell that by his occasional questions. In fact, he was so long in reading that Manny asked crossly if he was trying to memorize the script, adding that we didn't have the whole goddamned evening to spend at his stupid house. Pat Aloe told her mildly to shut her goddamned mouth and went back to his reading.

I had long since become used to Manny's occasionally salty talk and learned that I was not privileged to respond in kind. But Pat clearly was not taking orders from her. Despite his air of easygoing geniality, he was very much in command of Aloe activities. And, I was to find, he tolerated no violation of his authority.

When he had finished the last page of my manuscript, he put it with the others and returned them all to their envelope. Then he removed his reading glasses, thoughtfully massaged the bridge of his nose, and at last turned to me with a sober nod.

"You're a good man, Britt. It's a good job."

"Thank you," I said. "Thank you, very much."

Manny said words were cheap. How about a bonus for me? But Pat winked at her and waved her to silence.

"Y'know, Britt, I thought this deal would turn out the same kind of frammis that Manny's husband pulled. Banging the bejesus out of her and pissing off on the work. But I'm glad to admit I was wrong. You're A-OK, baby, and I'll swear to it on a stack of Bibles!"

Fortunately, I didn't have to acknowledge the compliment—such as it was—since Manny had begun cursing him luridly after his overripe appraisal of her late husband. Pat's booming laugh drowned out her protest.

"Ain't she a terror though, Britt? Just like the rest of her family, when she had a family. Her folks didn't speak to mine for years, just because my pop married an Irisher."

"Just don't you forget that bonus," Manny said. "You do and it'll be your big red ass."

"Hell, take care of it yourself," Pat said. "Make her come across heavy, Britt, baby. Hear me?"

I mumbled that I would do it. Grinning stiffly, feeling awkward and embarrassed to a degree I had never known before. He walked out of the library between the two us, a hand on each of our shoulders. Then, when we were at the door and had said our good-night, he laughingly roared that he expected me to collect heavy loot from Manny.

"Make her mind, Britt. 'S only kind of wife to have. Tell her you won't marry her until she comes through with your bonus!"

Marry her?

Marry her!

Well, what did I expect?

I tottered out of the house with Manny clinging possessively to my arm. And there was a coldish lump in my throat, a numbing chill in my spine.

We got in the car, and I drove away. Manny looked at me speculatively and asked why I was so quiet. And I said I wasn't being quiet, and then I said, What was wrong with being quiet? Did I have to talk every damned minute to keep her happy?

Ordinarily, popping off to her like that would have gotten me a chewing out or maybe a sharp slap. But tonight she said soothingly that of course I could be silent whenever I chose, because whatever I chose was also her choice.

"After all, we're a team, darling. Not two people, but a *couple*. Maybe we have our little spats, but there can't be any serious division between us."

I groaned. I said, "Oh, my God, Manny! Oh, Mary and Jesus and his brother, James!"

"What's the matter, Britt? Isn't that the way you feel?"

What I felt was that I was about to do something wholly irrelevant and unconstructive. Like soiling my clothes. For I was being edged closer and closer to the impossible. I mumbled something indistinguishable—something noncommittally agreeable. Because I knew now that I had to keep talking. Only in talk, light talk, lay safety.

Luckily, Manny indirectly threw me a cue by pushing the stole back from her shoulders and stretching her legs out in front of her. An action that tantalizingly exhibited her gold lamé evening gown; very short, very low-cut, very tight-seeming on her small, ultrafull body.

"It looks like it was painted on you," I said. "How in the world did you get into it?"

"Maybe you'll find out"—giving me a look. "After all, you have to take it off of me."

"We shall see," I said, desperate for words. For any kind of light talk. "We shall certainly see about this."

"Well, hurry up, for gosh sake! I've got to pee."

"Oh, my God," I said. "Why didn't you go before we left the house?"

"Because I needed help with my dress, darn it!"

I got her to the place. The place that had become *our* place.

I got her up the room and out of her clothes and onto the sink.

With no time to spare, either.

She cut loose and continued to let go at length. Sighing happily with the simple pleasure of relieving herself. She was such an earthy little thing, and I suppose few things are as good as a good leak when one has held in to the bursting point.

Talking, talking. Even after we were in bed and she was pressed tightly against me in orgasmic surgings.

9

I was physically ill by the time I got home that night. Sick with fear that the subject of marriage would be raised again, that it would be tossed to me like a ball, and that I would not be allowed to bat it aside or let it drop.

Repeatedly, I staggered out of my bed and went to the bathroom. Over and over, I went down on my knees and vomited into the bowl. Gagging up the bile of fear, I shivered and sweated with its burning chill. I tried to blame it on an overactive imagination, but I couldn't lie to myself. I'd lied once too often when I lied to Manny—about the one thing I should never have lied about. And the fact that the lie was one of omission, rather than commission, and that lying was more or less a way of life with me would not lift me off the hook a fraction of an inch. Not with Manuela Aloe. She would regard my lie as inexcusable—as, of course, it was.

In saying that I was unmarried on my PXA loan application, I hadn't meant to harm anyone. (I have never meant to harm anyone with what I did and didn't do.) It was just a way of avoiding trouble-some questions re the status of my marriage: were my wife and I living together; and if not, why not; and so on.

But I knew that Manny depended on that application for her information about me. And I could have and should have set her straight. For I knew—must have known—that I was not being treated with such extravagant generosity to buy Manny a passing relationship. She wanted a husband. One with good looks, good breeding, and a good name—the kind not easily found in her world or any world. Then she had found me and oh so clearly demonstrated the advantages of marriage to her, and I, tacitly, had agreed to the marriage. She had been completely honest with me, and I had been just as completely dishonest with her. And, now, by God—!

Now? . . .

But a man can be afraid just so much. (I say that as an expert on being afraid.) When he reaches that limit, he can fear no more. And so, at last, my pajamas wet with cold sweat, I returned to bed and fell into restless sleep.

In the morning, Mrs. Olmstead brought me toast and coffee and asked suspiciously if I had mailed a letter she had given me yesterday. I said that I had, for she was always giving me letters to mail, and I always remembered to mail. Or almost always. She nagged me, with increasing vehemence, about the imminent peril of rats. And I swore I would do something about them, too; and, mumbling and grumbling, she at last left me alone.

I lay back down and closed my eyes . . . *and Manny*

came into my room, a deceptive smile on her lovely face. For naturally, although she had learned that I was married, she showed no sign of displeasure.

"But it's all right, darling, and I understand perfectly. You needed the money, and you were dying to sleep with me. And—here, have a drink of this nice coffee I fixed for you."

"No! It's poisoned, and—yahh!"

"Oh, I'm so sorry, dear! I wouldn't have spilled it on you for the world. Let me just wipe it off—"

"Yeow! You're scratching my eyes out! Get away, go away . . . !"

My eyes snapped open.

I sat up with a start.

Mrs. Olmstead was bent over me. "My goodness, goodness me!" she exclaimed. "What's the matter, Mr. Rainstar?"

"Nothing; must've been having a nightmare," I said sheepishly. "Was I making a lot of racket?"

"Were you ever! Sounded like you was scared to death." Shaking her head grumpily, she turned toward the door. "Oh, yeah, your girlfriend wants you."

"What?" I said.

"Reckon she's your girlfriend, the way you're always pawing at each other."

"But—you mean Miss Aloe?" I stammered. "She's here?"

"Course she's not here. Don't see her, do you?" She gestured exasperatedly. "Answer the phone, afore she hangs up!"

I threw on a robe and ran downstairs.

I grabbed up the phone and said hello.

"Boo, you pretty man!" Manny laughed teasingly. "What's the matter with you, anyway?"

"Matter?" I said. "Uh, what makes you think anything's the matter?"

"I thought you sounded rather gruff and strained. But never mind. I want to see you. Be at our place in about an hour, okay?"

I swallowed heavily. Had she decided that something was wrong? That I was hiding something?

"Britt? . . ."

"Why?" I said. "What did you want to see me about?"

"What?" I could almost see her frown. "What did I want to see you *about*?"

I apologized hastily. I said I'd just gone to sleep after tossing and turning all night, and I seemed to be coming down with the flu. "I'd love to see you, Manny, child, but I think it would be bad for you. The way I'm feeling, the farther you keep away from me the better."

She said "Oh" disappointedly but agreed that it was probably best not to see me. She was leaving town for a couple of weeks—some business for Uncle Pat. Naturally, she would have liked a session with me before departing. But since I seemed to be coming down with something, and it wouldn't do for her to catch it. . . .

"You just take care of yourself, Britt. Get to feeling hale and hearty again, because you'll have to be when I get back."

"I'll look forward to it," I said. "Have a good trip, baby."

"And, Britt. I put a two-thousand-dollar bonus check in the mail to you."

"Oh, that's too much," I said. "I'm really overpaid as it is, and—"

"You just shut up!" she said sternly, then laughed. "Bye, now, darling. I gotta run."

"Bye to you," I said. And we hung up.

I had sent Connie three thousand dollars out of my first PXA check and another three out of the second, explaining that I'd gotten on to something good, though probably temporary, and that I'd send her all I could as long as it lasted. After all, I hadn't sent much before, lacking much to send, and it was a sort of conscience salve for my affair with Manny.

When my bonus arrived, I mailed Connie a check for the full two thousand. Then, after waiting a few days, until I was sure she had got it, I called her.

Britt Rainstar, stupe deluxe, figured that getting so much scratch—eight grand in less than two months— would put her in a fine mood. Bonehead Britt, sometimes known as the Peabrain Pollyanna, reasoned that all that loot would buy reasonableness and tolerance from Connie. Which just goes to show you. Yessir, that shows you, and it shows something about him, too. (*And please stop laughing, dammit!*)

For she was verbally leaping all over me, almost before I had asked her how she was feeling.

"I want to know where you got that money, Britt. I want to know how much more you got—a full and complete accounting, as Daddy says. And don't tell me that you got it from Hemisphere, because we've already talked to them and they said that you didn't. They said that you had severed your association with them. So you tell me where you're getting the money and exactly how much you're getting. Or, by golly, you'll wish you had."

"I see," I said numbly, surprised, though God knows I should not have been. I was always surprised, when being stupid, that people thought I was stupid. "I think I really see for the first time, namely that you and your daddy are a couple of miserable piles of shit."

"Who from and how much? I either find out from you, Mister Britton Rainstar, or—*What*? What did you say to me?"

"Never mind," I said. "I tell you the source of the money, and you check to see if I'm telling the truth— as to the quantity, that is. That's your plan, isn't it?"

"Well. . . ." She hesitated. "But I have a right to know! I'm your wife."

"Do you and are you?" I said. "A wife usually trusts her husband when he treats her as generously as I've been treating you."

That made her hesitate again, brought her to a still-longer pause.

"Well, *all right*," she said at last, grudgingly defensive. "I certainly don't want to make you lose your job, and . . . and . . . well, Hemisphere had no right to get huffy about it! Anyway, just look at what you did to me!"

"I didn't do anything to you, Connie. It was an accident."

"Well, anyway," she said. "Just the same!"

I didn't say anything. Simply waited. After a long silence, I heard her take a deep breath, and she spoke with an incipient sob.

"I s-suppose you want a divorce now. You wouldn't talk to me this way if you didn't."

"Divorce makes sense, Connie. You'll get just as much money, as if we were married, and I know you can't feel any great love for me."

"Then *you* do want a divorce?"

"Yes. It's the best thing for both of us, and—"

"WELL, YOU JUST TRY AND GET ONE!" she yelled. "I'll have you in jail for attempted murder so fast, it'll make your head swim! You arranged that accident that almost killed me, and the case isn't closed yet! They're ready to reopen it anytime Daddy and I say the word. And, golly, you try and get a divorce, and, by gosh—!"

"Connie," I said. "You surely can't mean that!"

"You'll see! You'll see if I don't. Just let me hear one more word out of you about a divorce, and . . . and . . . *I'll show you who's a pile of shit!*"

She slammed the phone down, completing any damage to my eardrum that had not been accomplished by her banshee scream. Of course, I'd hardly expected her to bedeck me with a crown of olive leaves or to release a covey of white doves to flutter about my head. But a threat to have me prosecuted for attempted murder was considerably more than I *had* expected.

At any rate, a divorce was impossible unless she agreed to it. Which meant that it was impossible period. Which meant that I could not marry Manny. Which meant? . . .

10

She, Manny, was back in town two weeks later, and she called me immediately upon her arrival. She suggested that I pick her up at the airport and go immediately to our place. I suggested that we have dinner and a talk before we did anything else. So, a little puzzled and reluctant, she agreed to that.

The restaurant was near the city waterworks lake. There was only a handful of patrons in it, this early-evening hour, and they gradually drifted out as I talked to Manny, apologizing and explaining. Explaining the inexplicable and apologizing for the inexcusable.

Manny said not a word throughout my recital—merely stared at me expressionlessly over her untouched dinner.

At last, I had nothing more to say, if I had ever had anything to say. And then, finally, she spoke, pulling a fringed silk shawl around her shoulders and rising to her feet.

"Pay the check and get out of here."

"What? Oh, well, sure," I said, dropping bills on the table as I also stood up. "And, Manny, I want you to know that—"

"Get! March yourself out to the car!"

We got out of the restaurant, with Manny clinging

to my arm, virtually propelling me by it. She helped *me* into the car, instead of vice versa. Then she got in, into the rear, sitting immediately behind me.

I heard her purse snap open. She said, "I've got a gun on you, Britt. So you get out of line just a little bit and you won't like what happens to you."

"M-Manny," I quavered. "P-please don't—"

"Do you know where I went while I was out of town?"

"N-no."

"Do you want to know what I did?"

"Uh, n-no," I said. "I don't think I do."

"Start driving. You know where."

"But—you mean our place? W-why do you want to—"

"*Drive!*"

I drove.

We reached the place. She made me walk ahead of her, inside and up the stairs and into our room.

I heard the click of the door lock. And then Manny asked if I'd heard a woman being slapped on the first day I went to her office.

I said that I had—or, rather, a recording of same; I had grown calmer by now, with a sense of fatalism.

"You heard *her*, Britt. She left the office by my private elevator."

I nodded, without turning around. "You wanted me to hear her. It was arranged, like the scene with Albert after you'd left that night. I was being warned that I'd better fly straight or else."

"You admit you *were* warned, then?"

"Yes. I tried to kid myself that it was all an unfortunate accident. But I knew better."

"But you went right ahead and deceived and cheated me. Did you really think I'd let you get away with it?"

I shook my head miserably, said I wanted to make things right insofar as I could. I'd give the car back and what little money I had left. And I'd sell everything I owned—clothes, typewriter, books, everything—to raise the rest. Anything she or PXA had given me, I'd give back, and—and—

"What about all the screwing I gave you? I suppose you'll give that back, too!"

"No," I said. "I'm afraid I can't do anything about that."

"Oh, sure you can," she said. "You can give me a good one right now."

And I whirled around, and she collapsed in my arms, laughing.

"Ahhh, Britt, darling! If you could have seen your face! You were really frightened, weren't you? You really thought I was angry with you, didn't you?"

"Of course I thought it!" I said, and, hugging her, kissing her, I swatted her bottom. "My God! The way you were talking and waving that gun around—!"

"Gun? Look, no gun!" She held her purse open for examination. "I couldn't be angry with you, Britt. What reason would I have? You were married, and you couldn't get unmarried. But you just about had to have the job, and you wanted me. So you did the only thing you could. I understand perfectly, and don't you give it another thought, because nothing is changed.

We'll go on just like we were; and everything's all right."

It was hard to believe that things would be all right. Knowing her as well as I did, I didn't see how they could be. As the weeks passed, however, my suspicions were lulled—almost, *almost* leaving me—for there was nothing whatsoever to justify them. I even found the courage to criticize her about her language, pointing out that it was hardly suitable to one with two college degrees. I can't say that it changed anything, but she acknowledged the criticism with seeming humility and solemnly promised to mend her ways.

So everything *was* all right—ostensibly. The work went on and went well. Ditto for my relationship with Manny. No one could have been more loving or understanding. Certainly no one, no other woman, had ever been as exciting. Over and over, I told myself how lucky I was to have such a woman. A wildly sensuous, highly intelligent woman who also had money and was generous with it, thus freeing me from the niggling and nagging guilt feelings that had heretofore hindered and inhibited me.

It is a fallacy that people who do not obtain the finer things in life have no appreciation for them. Actually, no one likes good things more than a bum— and I say this, knowing whereof I speak. I truly appreciated Manny after all the sorry b-axes that had previously been my lot. I truly appreciated everything she gave me, all the creature comforts she made possible for me, in addition to herself.

Everything wasn't just all right, as she had promised. Hell, everything was beautiful.

Until today.

The Day of the Dog....

I lay on my back, bracing myself against any movement that would cause him to attack.

I ached hideously, then grew numb from lack of movement; and shadows fell on the blinded windows. It was late afternoon. The sun was going down, and now—*my legs jerked convulsively*. They jerked again, even as I was trying to brace them. And now I heard a faint rustling sound: the dog tensing himself, getting ready to spring.

"D-don't! Please don't!"

Laughter. Vicious, maliciously amused laughter.

I rubbed my eyes with a trembling hand, brushed the blinding sweat from them.

The dog was gone. The manager of the place, the mulatto woman, stood at the foot of the bed. She jerked a thumb over her shoulder in a contemptuous gesture of dismissal.

"All right, prick. Beat it!"

"W-what?" I sat up shakily. "What did you say?"

"Get out. Grab your rags and drag ass!"

"Now, listen, you—you can't—"

"I can't what?"

"Nothing," I said. "If you'll just leave, so that I can get dressed...."

She said I'd get dressed while she was there, by God, because she wanted to look at the bed before I left. She figured a yellow bastard like me had probably shit in it. (*And where had I heard such talk before—the unnerving, ego-smashing talk of terror?*)

"Jus' so damned scared," she jeered. "Prob'ly shit the bed like a fucking baby. You did, I'm gonna make you clean it up."

I got dressed, with her watching.

I waited, head hanging like a whipped animal, while she jerked the sheets back, examined them, and then sniffed them.

"Okay," she said at last. "Reckon you got all your shit in you. Still full of it, like always."

I turned and started for the door.

"Don't you never come back, hear? I see your skinny ass again, I lays a belt on it!"

I got out of the place—so fast that I fell rather than walked down the stairs, almost crashed through the street door in attempting to open it the wrong way.

After the dog, I had thought nothing more could be done to me, that I was as demoralized as a man could get. But I was wrong. The vicious abuse of the mulatto woman had shaken me in a way that fear could not. Or perhaps it was the fear and the abuse together.

I drove blindly for several minutes, oblivious to the hysterical horn blasts of other cars, the outraged shouts of their drivers, and the squealing of brakes. Finally, however, when I barely escaped a head-on collision with a truck, I managed to pull myself together sufficiently to turn in to the curb and park.

I was on an unfamiliar street, one that I could not remember. I was stopped in front of a small cocktail lounge. Wiping my face and hands dry of sweat, I combed my hair and went inside.

"Yes, sir?" The bartender beamed in greeting, pushing a bowl of pretzels toward me. "What'll it be, sir?"

"I think I'll have a—"

I broke off at the sudden insistent jangling from a rear telephone booth. The bartender nodded toward it apologetically and said, "If you'll excuse me, sir? . . ." And I told him to go ahead.

He hurried from behind the bar and back to the booth. He entered and closed the door. He remained inside for two or three minutes. Then he came back, again stood in front of me.

"Yes, sir?"

"A martini," I said. "Very dry. Twist instead of olive."

He mixed the drink, poured it with a flourish. He punched numbers on the tabulating cash register, extended a check as he placed the glass before me.

"One fifty, sir. You pay now."

"Well—" I hesitated, shrugged. "Why not?"

I handed him two dollar bills. He said, "Exact change, sir."

And he picked up the drink and threw it in my face.

11

He was a lucky man. As I have said, my general easygoing and ah-to-hell-with-it attitude is marred by an occasional brief but violent flare-up. And if I had not been so completely beaten down by the dog and the mulatto woman, he would have gotten a broken arm.

But, of course, he had known I had nothing to strike back with. Manny, or the person who had made the call for her, had convinced him of the fact. Convinced him that he could pick up a nice piece of change without the slightest danger to himself.

I ran a sleeve across my face. I got up from my stool, turned, and started to leave. Then I stopped and turned back around, gave the bartender a long, hard stare. I wasn't capable of punching him, but there was something that I could do. I could make sure that there was a connection between the thrown drink and the afternoon's other unpleasantries—that, briefly, his action was motivated and not mere coincidence.

"Well?" His eyes flickered nervously. "Want somethin'?"

"People shouldn't tell you to do things," I said, "that they're afraid to do themselves."

"Huh? What're you drivin' at?"

"You mean, that was your own idea? You weren't paid to do it?"

"Do what? I don't know what you're talkin' about."

"All right," I said. "I'll tell some friends of mine what a nice guy you are."

I nodded coldly, again turned toward the door.

"Wait!" he said. "Wait a minute—uh—sir? It was a joke, see? Just a joke. I wasn't s'posed t' tell ya, an'— I can't tell ya nothin' else! I just *can't!* But—but—"

"It's all right," I said. "You don't need to."

I left the bar.

I drove home.

I parked in the driveway near the porch. Another car wheeled up behind mine, and Manny got out, smiling gaily as she came trotting up to me and hooked an arm through mine.

"Guess what I've got for you, darling. Give you three guesses!"

"A cobra," I said, "and two stink bombs."

"Silly! Let's go inside, and I'll show you."

"Let's," I said grimly, "and I'll show *you*."

We went up the steps and across the porch, Manny hugging my arm, smiling up into my face. The very picture of a woman with her love. Mrs. Olmstead heard us enter the house and hurried in from the kitchen.

"My, my!" She chortled, beaming at Manny. "I swear you get prettier every day, Miss Aloe."

"Oh, now." Manny laughed. "I couldn't look half as nice as your dinner smells. Were you inviting me to stay—I hope?"

"Course I'm inviting you! You betcha!" Mrs. Olmstead nodded vigorously. "You an' Mr. Rainstar just set yourself right down, an'—"

"I'm not sure I'll be here for dinner," I said. "I suspect that Miss Aloe won't be, either. Please come upstairs, Manuela."

"But looky here, now!" Mrs. Olmstead protested. "How come you ain't eatin' dinner? How come you let me go to all the trouble o' fixin' it if you wasn't going to eat?"

"I'll explain later. Kindly get up those stairs, Manuela."

I pointed sternly. Manny preceded me up the stairs, and I stood aside, waving her into my bedroom ahead of me. Then I closed and locked the door.

I was trembling a little—shaking with the day's pent-up fear and frustration, its fury and worry. Inwardly, I screamed to strike out at something, the most tempting target being Manny's plump little bottom.

So I wheeled around, my palm literally itching to connect with her flesh. But instead, Manny's soft mouth connected with mine. She had been waiting on tiptoe, waiting for me to turn. And now, having kissed me soundly, she urged me down on the bed and sat down at my side.

"I don't blame you for being miffed with me, honey. But I really couldn't help it. I honestly couldn't, Britt!"

"You couldn't, hmm?" I said. "You own the place, and that orange-colored bitch works for you, but you couldn't—"

"Wh-aat?" She stared at me incredulously. "Own it—our place, you mean? Why, that's crazy! Of course I don't own it, and that woman certainly does not work for me!"

"But, dammit to hell—! Wait a minute," I said. "What did you mean when you said you didn't blame me for being miffed with you?"

"Well . . . I thought that was why you were angry. Because I didn't come back from the bathroom."

"Oh," I said. "Oh, yeah. Why didn't you, anyway?"

"Because I couldn't, that's why. I had a little problem, one of those girl things, and it had to be taken care of in a hurry. . . ." So she'd hailed a cab and headed for the nearest drugstore. But it didn't have what she needed, and she'd had to visit two other stores before she found one that did. And by the time she'd returned to our place and taken care of the problem. . . .

"You might have waited, Britt. If you'd only waited and given me a chance to explain—but never mind." She took a three-thousand-dollar check from her purse and handed it to me. "Another bonus for you, dear." She smiled placatingly. "Isn't that nice?"

"Very," I said, folding it and tucking it in my pocket. "I'm going to keep it."

"Keep it? Why, of course you are. I—"

"I'm keeping the car, too," I said.

"Why not? It's your car."

"But my employment with PXA is finished as of right now. And if you want to know why—as if you didn't already know!—I'll tell you," I said. "And if I catch any more crap like I caught today, I'll tell you what I'll do about that, too!"

I told her in detail—the why and the what—with suitable embellishments and flourishes. I told her in more detail than I had planned and with considerable ornamentation. For while she heard me out in silence and without change of expression, I had a strong hunch that she was laughing at me.

When I had at last finished, out of breath and vituperation, she looked at me silently for several moments. Then she shrugged and stood up.

"I'll run along now. Good-bye and good luck."

I hadn't expected that. I don't know what I had expected, but not that.

"Well, look," I said. "Aren't you going to say anything?"

"I said good-bye and good luck. I see no point in saying anything else."

"But—dammit—! Well, all right!" I said. "Good-bye and good luck to you. And take your stinking bonus check with you!"

I thrust it on her—shoved it into her hand and folded her fingers around it. She left the room, and I hesitated, feeling foolish and helpless, that I had made a botch of everything. Then I started after her, stoping short as I heard her talking with Mrs. Olmstead.

"... loved to have dinner with you, Mrs. Olmstead. But in view of Mr. Rainstar's attitude. . . ."

"... just mean, he is! Accused me of bein' sloppy. Says I'm always sprinklin' rat poison on everything. O' course, I don't do nothin' of the kind. . . ."

"He should be grateful to you! Most women would leave at the sight of a rat."

"Well . . . just a minute, Miss Aloe. I'll walk you to your car."

It was several minutes before Mrs. Olmstead came back into the house. I waited until I heard her banging around in the kitchen, then went cautiously down the stairs and moved on tiptoe toward the front door.

"Uh-hah!" Her voice arrested me. "Whatcha sneakin' out for? Ashamed because you was so nasty to Miss Aloe?"

She had been lurking at the side of the staircase, out of sight from the upstairs. Apparently she had rushed in and hidden there after making the racket in the kitchen.

"Well?" She grinned at me with mocking accusation, hands on her skinny old hips. "Whatcha got to say for yourself?"

"What am I sneaking out for?" I said. "What have I got to say for myself? Why, goddammit—!" I stormed toward the door, cursing and fuming, ashamed and more furious with myself than I was with her. "And another thing!" I yelled. "Another thing, Mrs. Olmstead! You'd better remember what your position is in this house if you want to keep it!"

"Now you're threatenin' me." She began to sob noisily. "Threatenin' a poor old woman! Just as mean as you can be, that's what you are!"

"I'm not either mean!" I said. "I don't know how to be mean, and I wouldn't be if I did know how. I don't like mean people, and—goddammit, will you stop that goddam bawling?"

"If you wasn't mean, you wouldn't always forget to mail my letters! I found another one this mornin' when I was sending your clothes to the cleaners! I told you it was real important, an'—!"

"Oh, God, I *am* sorry," I said. "Please forgive me, Mrs. Olmstead."

I ran out the door and down the steps. But she was calling to me before I could get out of earshot.

"Your dinner, Mr. Rainstar. It's all ready and waiting."

"Thank you very much," I said. "I'm not hungry now, but I'll eat some later."

"It'll be all cold. You better eat now."

"I'm not hungry now. I've had a bad day, and I want to take a walk before I eat."

There was more argument, much more, but she finally slammed the door.

Not that I ever felt much like eating Mrs. Olmstead's cooking, but I certainly had no appetite for it tonight. And, of course, I felt guilty for not wanting to eat and having to tell her that I didn't. Regardless of whether something is my fault—and why should I have to eat if I didn't want to?—I always feel that I am in the wrong.

Along with feeling guilty, I was worried. About what Manny had done or had arranged to have done, its implications of shrewdness and power. And the fact that I had figuratively flung three thousand dollars in her face, as well as cutting myself off from all further income. At the time, I had felt that I had to do it. But what about the other categorical imperative that faced me? What about the absolute necessity to send money to Connie? To do it or else?

Well, balls to it, I thought, mentally throwing up my hands. I had told Mrs. Olmstead that I wanted to take a walk, so I had better be doing it.

I took a stroll up and down the road, a matter of a hundred yards or so. Then I walked around to the rear of the house and the weed-grown disarray of the backyard.

A couple of uprights of the gazebo had rotted away,

allowing the roof to topple until it was standing almost on edge. The striped awning of the lawn swing hung in faded tatters, and the seats of the swing lay splintered in the weeds where the wind had tossed them. The statuary—the little that hadn't been sold—was now merely fragmented trash, gleaming whitely in the night.

The fountain, at the extreme rear of the yard, had long since ceased to spout. But in the days when water poured from it, the ever-thirsting weeds and other rank growths had flourished into a minuscule jungle. And the jungle still endured, all but obscuring the elaborate masonry and piping of the fountain.

I walked toward it absently, somehow reminded of Goldsmith's "Deserted Village."

Reaching the periphery of the ugly overgrowth, I thought I heard the gurgling trickle of water. And, curious, I parted the dank and dying tangle with my hands and peered through the opening.

Inches from my face, eyeless eyes peered back at me. The bleached skull of a skeleton.

We stared at each other, each seemingly frozen in shock.

Then the skeleton raised a bony hand and leveled a gun at me.

12

I suddenly came alive. I let out a yell and flung myself to one side.

With my letting go of it, the overgrowth closed in

front of the skeleton. And as he pawed through it, I scrambled around to the rear of the fountain. There was cover that way, a shield from my frightful pursuer. But that way was also a trap.

The skeleton was between me and the house. Looming behind me, in the moonlit dimness, was the labyrinthine mass, the twisting hills and valleys, of the garbage dump.

I raced toward it, knowing that it was a bad move, that I was running away from possible help. But I continued to run. Running—fleeing—was a way of life with me. Buying temporary safety, regardless of its long-term cost.

Nearing the immediate environs of the garbage mounds, I began to trip and stumble over discarded bottles and cans and other refuse. Once my foot came down hard on a huge rat. And he leaped at me, screaming with pain and rage. Once, when I fell, a rat scampered inside of my coat, clawing and scratching as he raced over my chest and back. And I screamed and beat at myself long after I was rid of him.

There was a deafening roar in my ears: the thunder of my overexerted heart and lungs. I began to sob wildly in fear-crazed hysteria, but the sound of it was lost to me.

I crawled-clawed-climbed up a small mountain of refuse and fell tumbling and stumbling down the other side. Broken bottles and rotting newspapers and stinking globs of food came down on top of me, along with the hideously bloated body of a dead rat. And I swarmed up out of the mess and continued my staggering, wobble-legged run.

I ran down the littered lanes between the garbage hillocks. I ran back up the lanes. Up, down, down, up. Zigzagging, repeatedly falling and getting to my feet. And going on and on and on. Fleeing through this lonely stinking planet, this lost world of garbage.

I dared not stop. For I was pursued, and my pursuer was gaining on me. Getting closer and closer with every passing moment.

Thoroughly in the thrall of hysteria, I couldn't actually see or hear him. Not in the literal meaning of the words. It was more a matter of being made aware of certain things, of having them thrust upon my consciousness: a discarded bottle rolling down a garbage heap, or a heavy shadow falling over my own, or hurrying footsteps splashing up a spray of filth.

At last I tottered to the top of a long hummock and down the other side.

And there he—it—was. Grabbing me from behind. Wrapping strong arms around me and holding me helpless.

I screamed, screams that I could not hear.

I struggled violently, fear giving me superhuman strength. And I managed to break free.

But for only a split second.

Then an arm went around my head, holding it motionless—a target. And then a heavy fist came up—swung in a short, swift arc—and collided numbingly with my chin.

And I went down, down, down.
Into darkness.

13

At the time of the accident, Connie and I had been
married about six months. I had been at work all day
on an article for a teachers' magazine, and I came
down into the kitchen that evening, tired and hungry,
to find Connie clearing away the dirty dishes.

She said she and her father had already eaten, and
he'd gone back to his office. She said there were some
people in this world who had to work for a living, even
if I didn't know it.

"I've been working," I said. "I've almost finished
my article."

"Never mind," she said. "Do you want some pancakes or something? There isn't any of the stew left."

"I'm sorry I didn't hear you call me for dinner. I
would have been glad to join you."

"Will you kindly tell me whether you want something to eat?" she yelled. "I'm worn out, and I don't
feel like arguing. It's just been work, work, work, from
the time I got up this morning. Cooking and sewing
and cleaning, and—and I even washed the car on top
of everything else!"

I said that she should never wash a car on top of
anything, let alone everything. Then, I said, "Sorry, I
would have washed the car. I told you I would."

She said oh, sure, a lot I would do. "Just look at you!

You can't even shine your shoes. You don't see my daddy going around without his shoes shined, and he *works*."

I looked at her. The spitefully glaring eyes, the shrewish thrust of her chin. And I thought, What the hell gives here, anyway? She and her papa had been increasingly nasty to me almost from the day we were married. But tonight's performance beat anything I had previously been subjected to.

"You and your daddy," I said, "are very, very lovely people. Strange as it may seem, however, your unfailing courtesy and consideration have not made a diet of pancakes and table scraps palatable to me. So I'll go into town and get something to eat, and you and your daddy can go burp in your bibs!"

I was heading for the door as I spoke, for Connie had a vile temper and was not above throwing things at me or striking me with them.

I flung the door open, and—and there was a sickening *thud* and a pained scream from Connie, a scream that ended almost as soon as it began. I turned around, suddenly numb with fear.

Connie lay crumpled on the floor. A deep crease, oozing slow drops of blackish blood, stretched jaggedly across her forehead.

She had been hit by the sharp edge of the door when I threw it open. She was very still, as pale as death.

I grabbed her up and raced out to the car with her. I placed her on the backseat and slid under the wheel. And I sent the car roaring down the lane from the house and into the road that ran in front of it. Or, rather, *across* the road, for I was going too fast to make the turn.

The turn was sharp, one that was dangerous even at relatively low speeds. I knew it was, as did everyone else in the area. And I could never satisfactorily explain why I was traveling as fast as I was.

I was unnerved, of course. And, of course, I had lost my head, as I habitually did when confronted with an emergency. But, still. . . .

Kind of strange for a man to do something when he danged well knew he shouldn't. Kind of suspicious.

The road skirted a steep cliff. It was almost three hundred feet from the top of the cliff to the bottom. The car went over it and down it.

I don't know why I didn't go over with it—as Connie did.

I couldn't explain. Nor could I explain why I was speeding when I hit the turn. Nor could I prove that I had hit Connie with the door accidentally instead of deliberately.

I was an outsider in a clannish little community, and it was known that I constantly bickered with my wife. And I was the beneficiary of her hundred-thousand-dollar life-insurance policy—two-hundred-thousand with the double indemnity.

If Connie's father hadn't stoutly proclaimed me innocent—Connie also defending me as soon as she was able—I suspect that I would have been convicted of attempted murder.

As I still might be—unless I myself was murdered.

14

The night of the skeleton, of my chase through the garbage dump. . . .

I was kept under sedation for the rest of that night and much of the next day and night. I had to be, so great was the damage to my nervous system. Early the following afternoon, after I had gotten some thirty-six hours of rest and treatment, Detective Sergeant Jeff Claggett was admitted to my hospital room.

It was Jeff who had followed me into the garbage dump, subsequently knocking me out when I could not be reasoned with. He had taken up the chase after hearing my yell and seeing my flight from the house. But he had seen no one pursuing me.

"I suppose no one was," I admitted, a little sheepishly. "I know he started around the fountain after me. But I was so damned sure that he was right on my tail that I didn't turn around to see if he was."

"Can't say that I blame you," Claggett said with a nod. "Must've given you a hell of a shock to come up against something like that pointing a gun at you. Any idea who it was?"

"No way of telling." I shook my head. "Just someone in a skeleton costume. You've probably seen them —a luminous skeleton painted on black cloth."

"Not much of a lead. Could've been picked up anywhere in the country," Claggett said. "Tell me, Britt. Do you walk around in your backyard as a regular thing? I mean, could the guy have known you'd be there at about such and such a time?"

"No way," I said. "I haven't been in the backyard in the last five years."

"Then he was just hiding there in the weeds, don't you suppose? Keeping out of sight, say, until he could safely come into the house."

"Come into the house?" I laughed shakily. "Why would he want to do that?"

"Well . . ." Jeff Claggett gave me a deadpan look. "Possibly he was after your money and valuables. After all, everyone knows you're a very wealthy man."

"You're kidding!" I said. "Anyone who knows anything about me knows that I don't have a pot to—"

"Right." He cut me off. "So what the guy was after was you. He'd have you pinned down in the house. You'd probably wake up—he'd wake you, of course—to find him bending over your bed. A skeleton grinning at you in the dark. You couldn't get away from him, and—yes? Something wrong, Britt?"

"Something *wrong!*" I shuddered. "What are you trying to do to me, Jeff?"

"Who hates you that much, Britt? And don't tell me you don't know!"

"But—but I don't," I stammered. "I've probably rubbed a lot of people the wrong way, but. . . ."

I broke off, for he was holding something in front of me, then dropping it on the bed with a grimace. A pamphlet bylined by me, with a line attributing sponsorship to PXA.

"That's why I came out to see you the other night, Britt. I ran across it in the library, and I was sure the

136

use of your name was unauthorized. But I guess I was wrong, wasn't I?"

I hesitated, unable to meet his straightforward blue eyes, their uncompromising honesty. I took a sip of water through a glass straw, mumbled a kind of defiant apology for my employment with PXA.

"It's nothing to be ashamed of, Jeff. It was a public-service thing. Nothing to do with the company's other activities."

"No?" Claggett said wryly. "Those activities paid for your work, didn't they? A lot more than it was worth, too, unless my information is all wrong. Three thousand dollars a month, plus bonuses, plus a car, plus an expense account, plus—let's see. What else was included in the deal? A very juicy—and willing—young widow?"

"Look," I said, red-faced. "What's this got to do with what happened to me?"

"Don't kid me, Britt. I've talked to her—her and her uncle both. It's normal procedure to inform a man's employers when he's had a mishap. So I had a nice little chat with them, and you know what I think?"

"I think you're going to tell me what you think."

"I think that Patrick Xavier Aloe had been expecting Manuela to visit some unpleasantness upon you and is now sure that she did. I think he gave her plenty of hell as soon as I left the office."

I thought the same, although I didn't say so. Claggett went on to reveal that he had talked with Mrs. Olmstead, learning, of course, that we were much more than employer and employee.

"She put out a lot of money for you, my friend. Or arranged to have it put out. She also put out something far more important to a girl like that. I imagine she only did it in the belief that you were going to marry her. . . ."

He waited, studying me. I nodded reluctantly.

"I should have known what was expected of me," I said. "Hell, maybe I did know but wouldn't admit it. At any rate, it was a lousy thing to do, and I probably deserve whatever she hands out."

"Oh, well." Claggett shrugged. "You weren't very nice to your wife, either."

"Probably not, but she's an entirely different case. Manny was good to me. I never got anything from Connie and her old man but a hard time."

"You say so, and I believe you," said Claggett warmly. "Any damage you do, I imagine, is the result of *not* doing—just letting things slide. You don't have the initiative to deliberately hurt anyone."

"Thanks," I said. "I guess."

He chuckled good-naturedly. "Tell me about Connie and her father. Tell me how you happened to marry her, since it obviously wasn't a love match."

I gave him a brief history of my meeting and association with the Bannermans. Then, since he seemed genuinely interested, I gave him a quick rundown on Britton Rainstar, after fortune had ceased to smile upon him and he had become, lo, the Poor Indian.

Jeff Claggett listened attentively—by turns laughing, frowning, exclaiming, wincing, and shaking his head. When I had finished, he said that I was obviously much tougher than he had supposed. I must be to survive the many messes I had gotten myself into.

"Just one damned thing after another!" he swore. "I don't know how the hell you could do it!"

"Join the crowd," I said. "Nobody has ever known how I did it. Including me."

"Well, getting back to the present. Miss Aloe expected you to marry her. How did she take the news that you couldn't?"

"A lot better than I had any right to expect," I said. "She was just too good about it to be true, if you know what I mean. Everything was beautiful for around six weeks, just as nice as it had been from the beginning. Then a couple of days ago, the day of the evening I jumped this character in the skeleton suit—"

"Hold it a minute. I want to write this down."

He took a notebook and pencil from his pocket, then nodded for me to proceed. I did so, telling him of the dog and the mulatto woman and the bartender who had thrown the drink in my face.

Jeff made a few additions to his notes when I had finished, then returned the book and pencil to his coat. Leaning back in his chair, he stared up at the ceiling meditatively, hands locked behind his head.

"Three separate acts," he said, musingly. "Four, counting the skeleton routine. But there's a connection between them. The tie-in is in the result of those acts. To give you a hard jolt when you least expect it."

"Yes," I said uneasily. "They certainly did that, all right."

"I wonder. I just wonder if that's how her husband died."

"You know about him?" An icy rill tingled down my spine. "She told me he died very suddenly, but I just assumed it was from a heart attack."

Claggett said that all deaths were ultimately attributable to heart failure, adding that he had no very sound arguments for regarding the death of Manny's husband as murder.

"They were at this little seacoast resort when it was hit by a hurricane. Wiped out almost half the town. Her husband was one of the dead. Wait, now—" He held up his hand as I started to speak. "Naturally, she couldn't have arranged the hurricane, but she could have used it to cover his murder. I'd say she had plenty of reason to want him out of the way."

"I gather that he wasn't much good," I said. "But—"

"She dropped out of sight right after the funeral. Disappeared without a trace, and she didn't show up again for about a year."

"Well?" I said. "I still don't see. . . ."

"Well, neither do I," Claggett said easily, his manner suddenly changing. "What are you going to do now, Britt, that you've quit the pamphlet writing?"

I said that I wished to God I knew. I wouldn't have any money to live on, and none to send Connie, which would surely cause all hell to pop. I was beginning to regret that I'd quit the job, even though I'd had no choice in the matter.

Claggett said I didn't have one now, either. I had to

go back on the job. "You'll be safer than if you didn't, Britt. So far, Miss Aloe's only given you a bad shaking up. But she might try for a knockout if she thinks you're getting away from her."

"We don't actually *know* that she's done anything," I said. "We think she's responsible, but we're certainly not sure."

"Right. And we never will be if you break completely with her. Not until it's too late."

"But I've already quit! And I made it pretty damned clear that I meant it!"

"But she didn't tell her uncle, apparently. Probably afraid of catching more hell than he's already given her." He stood up, dusting at his trousers. "I'll be having a little chat with both of them today, and I'll tip her off privately first—let her know that you're keeping the job. You can bet she'll be tickled pink to hear it."

The door opened and a bright-faced young nurse came in. She gave me a quick smile, then said something to Jeff that was too low for me to hear.

He nodded, dismissing her, and turned back to me. "Have to run, I guess," he said. "Okay? Everything all right?"

"Absolutely perfect," I said bitterly. "How else could it be for a guy with a schizoid wife and a paranoid girlfriend? If one of them can't send me to prison or the electric chair, the other will put me in the nuthouse or the morgue! Well, screw it." I plopped back on the pillows. "What are you chatting with the Aloes about?"

"Oh, this and that," he said with a shrug. "About you mainly, I suppose. They're very concerned about you and anxious to see you, of course. . . ."

"Of course!"

"So, if it's all right with you, I'll have them drop in around five."

15

There is something utterly unnerving about an absolutely honest man, a man like Sergeant Jeff Claggett. You rationalize and lie to him until your supply of deceit is exhausted; and his questions and comments are never brutal or blunt. He simply persists, when you have already had your say, looking at you when you can no longer look at him. And, finally, though nothing has been admitted, you know you have been in the fight of your life.

So I don't know what Jeff said that afternoon to Manuela and Patrick Xavier Aloe. It is likely that he was quite offhand and casual, that he said nothing at all of intrinsic significance. But they came into my room, a tinge of strain to their expressions, and Manny's lips seemed a little stiff as she stooped to kiss me.

I shook hands with Pat and stated that I was fine, just fine. They stated that that was fine, just fine, and that I was looking fine, just fine.

There was an awkward moment of silence after that, while I smiled at them and was smiled back at. Manny shattered the tension by bursting into giggles. They made her very nice to look at, shaking and shivering her in all her shakable, shivery parts.

Pulse pounding, I tentatively joined in her laughter. But Pat saw no cause for amusement.

"What's with you?" He glared at her. "We got a sick man here. He gets a damned stupid joke pulled on him, and it puts him in the hospital. You think that's funny?"

"Now, Uncle Pat. . . ." Manny gestured placatingly.

"Britt lands in the hospital, and we get cops nosing all around! Maybe you like that, huh? You think cops are funny?"

"There was only one, Pat. Just Sergeant Claggett, and he's a family friend, isn't he, Britt?"

"A very old friend," I said. "Jeff—Sergeant Claggett, that is—would be concerned regardless of why I was in the hospital."

"Well. . . ." Pat Aloe was somewhat reassured. "Anything else happen to you recently, Britt? I mean, any little jokes like this last one?"

I hesitated, feeling Manny's eyes on me. Wondering what Jeff would consider the best answer. Pat's gaze moved from me to Manny, and she smiled at him sunnily.

"Of course nothing else has happened to him, Pat. This is his first time in the hospital, isn't it?"

"That's right," I said, and then gave him the qualified truth. "There's been nothing like this before."

He relaxed at that, his map-of-Ireland face creasing

in a grin. He said he was damned glad to hear it, because they'd been getting A-OK reactions to the pamphlets, and he'd hate to see them loused up.

"And we'd hate to lose the tax write-off," Manny said. "Don't forget that, Uncle Pat."

"Shut up," Pat said, and to me, "Then everything's copacetic, right, Britt? You're gonna go right on working for us?"

"I'd like to," I said. "I understand that I'll be under medical supervision for a while, have to take things kind of easy. But if that's all right with you. . . ."

He boomed that, of course, it was all right. "And don't you worry about the hospital and doctor bills. We got kind of a private insurance plan that takes care of everything in the medical line."

"That's great," I said. "I'm obliged to you."

"Forget it. Whatever makes you happy, makes us happy, right, Manny? Anything that's jake with Britt —Britt and his friend, Sergeant Claggett—"

"Is jake with us," Manny said emphatically. "Right, Uncle Pat! Right on!"

And Pat shot her a warning look. "One more thing, Britt, baby. I was way out of line saying anything about you and Manny getting married. What the hell? That's your business, not mine."

"*Right!*" said Manny.

"You want a bat in the chops?" He half raised his hand. "Keep askin', and you're gonna get it."

I broke in to say quite truthfully that I would have been glad to marry Manny if I had been free to do so. Pat said, sure, sure, so who was kicking? "It's okay with me, and it's okay with her. She don't like it, she can shove it up her ass."

"Right back at you, you sawed-off son of a bitch," said Manny, and she made an upward jabbing motion with one finger.

Pat leaped. He grabbed her by the shoulders and shook her so vigorously that her head seemed to oscillate, her hair flying out from it in a golden blur. He released her with a shove that slammed her into the wall. And the noise of his angry breathing almost filled the room.

I felt a little sick. Savagery like this was something I had never seen before. As for Manny. . . .

Something indefinable happened to her face—a flickering of expressions that wiped it free of expression, then caused it to crinkle joyously, to wreathe itself in a cherubic smile.

Pat looked away, gruffly abashed. "Let's go." He jerked a thumb over his shoulder. "Get out of here, and let Britt get some rest."

"You go ahead," she said. "I want to kiss Britt good-night."

"Who's stopping you? You kissed him in front of me before."

"Huh-uh. Not this way I didn't."

He gave me an embarrassed glance, then shrugged and said he could stand it if I could. He told me to take it easy and left. And Manny crossed to the door, locked it, and come back to the bed. She looked down, then bent down so close that her breasts brushed against me.

"Go ahead," she whispered. "Grab a handful."

"Now, dammit, Manny! . . ." I tried to sit up. "Listen to me, Manny!"

"Look," edging her blouse down, "look how nice they are."

"I said *listen to me!*"

"Oh, all right," she said poutingly. "I'm listening."

"You've got to stop it," I said. "We'll forget what's already happened. Just say I had it coming and call it quits. But there can't be any more, understand? And don't ask me any more what!"

"Any more what?"

"Please," I said. "I'm trying to help you. If you'll just stop now. . . ."

"But I really don't know what you mean, darling. If you'll just tell me what you want me to stop, what else I shouldn't do. . . ."

"All right," I said. "I've done my best."

She studied me a moment, the tip of her finger in her mouth. Then she nodded, became pseudo-business-like, declared that she knew just what I needed, and it so happened that she had brought a supply with her.

As I have noted previously, she moved very, very quickly when she chose. So she was on the bed, on top of me, before I knew what was happening, smothering me with softness, moving against me sensuously.

There was an abrupt metallic squeal from the bed, then a grating and a scraping and a *crash*. Instinctively, I jerked my head up, so it did not smash against the hard hospital floor. But my neck snapped, painfully, and Manny helped me to my feet, murmuring apologies.

Someone was pounding on the door, noisily working at the lock. It opened suddenly, and the nurse came in, almost at a run. It was the nurse I had seen earlier, the bright-faced young woman. None too gently she brushed Manny aside and seated me comfortably in a chair. She felt my pulse and forehead, gave me a few fussy little pats. Then she turned on Manny, who was casually adjusting her clothes.

"Just what happened here, miss? Why was that door locked?"

Manny grinned at her impudently. "A broken-down bed and a locked door, and you ask me what *happened*? How long have you been a woman, dear?"

The nurse turned brick red. Her arm shot out, the finger at its end pointing sternly toward the door. "I want you out of here, Miss! Right this minute!"

"Oh, all right," Manny said. "Unless I can do something else for Britt. . . ."

"No," I said. "Please do as the nurse says, Manny."

She did so, lushly compact hips swinging provocatively. The nurse looked after her, a little downcast, I thought, as though doing some comparative weighing and finding herself sadly wanting.

An orderly removed the collapsed bed and wheeled in another. I was put into it, and a doctor examined me and pronounced me indestructible.

"Just the same," he said, winking at me lewdly, "you lay off the double sacking with types like that pocket

Venus that was in here. I'd say she could spot you a tail wind and still beat you into port."

"Oh, she could not," the nurse said, reddening gloriously the moment the words were out of her mouth. "How would you know, anyway?"

"We-ll. . . ." He gave her a wisely laconic grin. "How would *you*?"

He slapped unsuccessfully at her bottom on the way out. She jerked away, greatly flustered, and darted a glance at me. And, of course, she found nothing in my expression but earnest goodwill.

She was much prettier than I had thought at first glance. She had superb bone structure, and her hair, too austerely coiffed beneath her nurse's cap, was deep auburn.

"I don't believe I've seen you before today," I said. "Are you new on this floor?"

"Well. . . ." She hesitated. "I guess I'm new on all of them. I mean, I'm a substitute nurse."

"I see," I said. "Well, I think you're a fine nurse, and I'm sure you'll have regular duty before long."

She twitched pleasurably, like a petted puppy. Then her scrubbed-clean face fell, and she sighed heavily.

"I thought I was going to have steady work starting tomorrow," she said. "Steady for a while, anyway. But after what happened today—well, I'll be held responsible. The bed wouldn't have been broken down if I hadn't allowed the door to be locked. You could have been seriously injured, and it's all my fault, and—"

"Wait!" I held up a hand. "Hold it a minute. It wasn't your fault, it was mine, and I won't allow the hospital to blame you for it. You just have your supervisor talk to me, and I'll straighten her out fast."

"Thank you, Mr. Rainstar, but the supervisor has already reported the matter to Sergeant Claggett. She had to, you know. Her orders were to report anything unusual that happened to you. So. . . ."

I was the regular duty the nurse had hoped to have. The doctors felt that for a time at least, when I returned home, I should have a full-time nurse available. And she had seemed a likely candidate for the job. But Jeff Claggett would never approve of her now.

"I really blew it," she said, with unconscious humor. "I'll bet the sergeant is really disgusted with me."

I said loftily that she was to forget the sergeant. After all, I was the one who had to be satisfied, and she satisfied me in every respect, so she could consider herself hired.

"Oh, that's wonderful, just wonderful!" She wriggled delightedly. "You're sure Sergeant Claggett will approve?"

"If he doesn't, he'll have me to deal with," I said. "But I'm sure it'll be fine with him."

But I wasn't sure, of course. And, of course, it wasn't fine with him.

16

He returned to the hospital shortly after I had finished my dinner that evening. He had been busy since leaving me, checking at the cocktail lounge where I had gotten a drink in my face and with the mulatto woman who managed the quiet little hotel. In neither case had his investigation come to aught but naught.

The bartender had quit his job and departed town for parts unknown to the lounge owner. Or so, at least, the latter said. The hotel had the same owners it had always had—a large eastern realty company, which was the absentee landlord for literally hundreds of properties. The manageress owned no dog, denied any knowledge of one, and also denied that she had done anything but rent me and my "wife" a room.

"So that's that," Claggett said. "If you like, I can put out a John Doe warrant on the bartender, but I don't think it's worth the trouble. Assuming we could run him down, which I doubt, throwing a drink on you wouldn't add up to more than a misdemeanor."

"By itself," I said with a nod. "But when you add it on to the business with the dog, and—"

"How are you going to add it on? You're a married man, but you register into this hotel with another woman as Mr. and Mrs. Phoneyname. And you tied your hands right there. The manageress was lying, sure. But try to prove it and you'll look like a jerk."

He seemed rather cross and out of sorts. I suggested as much, adding that I hoped I wasn't the cause of same.

He gave me a look, seemed on the point of saying something intemperate. Then he sighed wearily and shook his head.

"I guess you just can't help it," he said tiredly. "You seem incapable of learning from experience. You know, or should know, that Miss Aloe is out to harm you. You don't know how far she intends to go, which makes her all the more dangerous to you. But you let her get rid of Pat, you let her lock the door, you let her come back to the bed and make certain adjustments to it—"

"Look," I protested. "She didn't do all those things separately with a time lapse between them. She's a very quick-moving little girl, and she did everything in a matter of seconds. Before I knew what was happening, she—" I broke off. "Uh, what do you mean, certain adjustments?" I said.

"The bed goes up and down, right? Depending on whether you want to sit up or sleep or whatever. And here, right here where I'm pointing—" He pointed. "Do you see it, that little lever?"

"I see it," I said.

"Well, that's the safety. It locks the bed into the position you put it in."

"I know," I said. "They explained that to me the first day I was here."

"That's good," Claggett said grimly. "That's real good. Well, if Miss Aloe was out to fracture your skull, she couldn't have had a more cooperative subject. You let her flip the safety and use her weight to give you an extra-hard bang against the floor. You didn't let her tie a rocket to you, but I imagine you would if she'd asked you."

My mouth was suddenly very dry. I took a sip or two of water, then raised the glass and drained it.

"I thought it was just a silly accident," I said. "It never occurred to me that she'd try anything here in the hospital."

"Well, watch yourself from now on," Claggett said. "You're going to be thrown together a lot, I understand, in the course of doing these pamphlets. Or am I correct about that?"

"Well. . . ." I shrugged. "That depends largely on Manny. She's calling the turns. The amount of time we spend together depends on her."

"Better count on more time with her than less, then," he said. "This little stunt she pulled today—well, I doubt that it was really a try for a knockout. Whenever she's ready for that, if she ever is ready, I think she'll stay in the background and have someone else do it."

I said yes, I supposed he was right. He made an impatient little gesture, as though I had said something annoying.

"But we can't be sure, Britt! We can't say what she might do since she probably doesn't know herself. Look at what's happened to you so far. She couldn't have planned those things. They've just been spur of the moment—pulled out of her hat as she went along."

I made no comment this time. He went on to say that he'd done some heavy thinking about Manny's vanishing for a year after her husband's death. And there was only one logical answer as to where she had been and why.

"A private sanitarium, Britt, a place where she could

get psychiatric help. Her mind started bending with the trouble her husband gave her, and it finally broke when he died—or when she killed him. I'd say that your telling her you were married was more than she could take, and it's started her on another mental breakdown."

"Well," I laughed nervously, "that's not a very comforting thought."

"You'll be all right as long as you're careful. Just watch yourself—and her. Think now. Everything that's happened to you so far has been at least partly your own fault. In a sense, you've set yourself up."

I gave that a moment's thought, and then I said all right, he was right. I would be very, very careful from now on. Since I had but one life to live, I would do everything in my power to go on living it.

"You have my solemn promise, Jeff. I shall do everything in *my* power to keep *myself* alive and unmaimed. Now, just what are you doing along that line?"

"I've done certain things inside your house," he said. "If there's ever any trouble, just let out a yell and you'll have help within a minute."

"How?" I said. "You mean you have the place bugged?"

"Don't try to find out," he said. "If you didn't know, Miss Aloe won't, and if you did, she would. You're really pretty transparent, Britt."

"Oh, now, I don't know about that," I said. "I—"

"Well, I *do* know. You're not only just about incapable of deceiving anyone for any length of time, but you're also very easy to deceive. So take my word for it that you'll be all right. Just yell and you'll have help."

"I don't like it," I said. "Suppose I couldn't yell? That I didn't have time or I wasn't allowed to?"

Claggett laughed, shook his head chidingly. "Now, Britt, be reasonable. You'll have a full-time nurse right in the house with you, and she'll be checking on you periodically. It's inconceivable that you could need help and be unable to get it."

It wasn't inconceivable to me. I could think of any number of situations in which I would need help and be unable to cry out for it. And, for the record, one of those situations *did* come about. It *did* happen, the spine-chilling, hair-raising occurrence I had most feared. And just when I was feeling safest and most secure. And I could see no way of hollering for help without hastening my already-imminent demise.

All I could do was lie quiet, as I was ordered to, and listen to my hair turn grayer still. Wondering, foolishly, if I could ever get an acceptable tint job on it, assuming that I lived long enough to need one.

But that is getting ahead of the story. It is something that was yet to happen. Tonight, the night of which I am writing, Claggett pointed out that he was only a detective sergeant and that as such there was a limit to what he could do for my protection.

"And I'm sure the arrangements I've made are enough, Britt. With you staying on the alert and with a good, reliable nurse on hand, I'm confident that—"

He broke off, giving me a sudden sharp look. "Yes?" he said. "Something on your mind?"

"Well, uh, yes," I said uncomfortably. "About the nurse. I'd like to have the one who's on duty tonight. That kind of pretty reddish-haired one. I . . . I, uh . . . I mean, she needs the job, and. . . ."

"Not a chance," Claggett said flatly. "Not in a thousand years. I've got another nurse in mind, an older woman. Used to be a matron at the jail a few years back. I'll have her come in right now, and you can be getting acquainted tonight."

He got up and started toward the door. I said, "Wait a minute."

He paused and turned around. "Well?"

"Well, I'd kind of like to have the reddish-haired girl. She wants the job, and I'm sure she'd be just fine."

"Fine for what?" Claggett said. "No, don't tell me. You just take care of golden-haired Miss Aloe and forget about your pretty little redhead."

I said I didn't have anything like that in mind at all—whatever it was he thought I had in mind. My God, with Connie and Manny to contend with, I'd be crazy to start anything up with another girl.

"So?" said Claggett, then cut me off with a knifing gesture of his hand as I began another protest. "I don't care if you did promise her the job. You had no right to make such a promise, and she knows it as well as you do."

He turned and stalked out of the room.

I expected him to be back almost immediately,

bringing the ex-police matron with him. But he was gone for almost a half an hour, and he came back looking wearily resigned.

"You win," he said, dropping heavily into a chair. "You get your red-haired nurse."

"I do?" I said. "I mean, why?"

"Because she spread it all around that she had the job. She was so positive about it that even the nurse I had in mind was convinced, and she got sore and quit."

"I'm sorry," I said. "I really didn't mean to upset your plans, Jeff."

"I know," he said with a shrug. "I just wish I could feel better about the redhead."

"I'm sure she'll work out fine," I said. "She got off to a bad start today by letting Manny lock the door and pull the bed trick. But—"

"What?" said Claggett. "Oh, well, that didn't bother me. That could have happened regardless of who was on duty. The thing that bothers me about Miss Redhead Scrubbed-Clean is that I can't check her out."

I said, "Oh," not knowing quite why I said it. Or why the hair on the back of my neck had gone through the motions of attempting to rise.

". . . raised on a farm," Jeff Claggett was saying. "No neighbors for miles around. No friends. Her parents were ex-teachers, and they gave her her schooling. They did a first-class job of it, too, judging by her entrance exams at nursing school. She scored an academic rating of high-school graduate plus two years of college. She was an honors graduate in nursing, and I can't turn up anything but good about her since she made RN. Still—" He shook his head troubledly. "I don't actually *know* anything about her for the first eighteen years of her life. There's nothing I can check on, not even a birth certificate, from the time she was born until she entered nurses' training."

A linen cart creaked noisily down the hallway. From somewhere came the crash of a dinner tray. (*Probably the redhead pounding on a patient.*)

"Look, Jeff," I said, "in view of what you've told me, and after much deliberation, I think I'd better have a different nurse."

"Not possible." Jeff shook his head firmly. "You promised her the job. I went along with your decision when I found that my matron friend wasn't and wouldn't be available. Try to back down on the deal now and we'd have the union on us."

"I'll tell you something," I said. "I find that I've undergone a very dramatic recovery. My condition has improved at least a thousand percent, and I'm not going to need a nurse at all."

Claggett complained that I hadn't been listening to him. I'd already engaged a nurse—the redhead—and the doctors said I *did* need one.

"I've probably got the wind up over nothing, anyway, Britt. After all, the fact that I can't check on her doesn't mean that she's hiding anything, now does it?"

"Yes," I said. "I think it's proof positive that she was up to no good during those lost years of her nonage and that she is planning more of same for me."

Claggett chuckled that I was kidding, that I was

always kidding. I said not so, that I only kidded when I was nervous or in mortal fear for my life, as in the present instance.

"It's kind of a defense mechanism," I explained. "I reason that I can't be murdered or maimed while would-be evildoers are laughing."

Claggett said brusquely to knock off the nonsense. He was confident that the nurse would work out fine. If he'd had any serious doubts about her, he'd've acted upon them.

"I'll have to go now, Britt. Have a good night, and I'll talk to you tomorrow."

"Wait!" I said. "What if I'm murdered in my sleep?"

"Then I won't talk to you," he said irritably.

And he left the room before I could say anything else.

I got up and went to the bathroom. The constant dryness of my mouth had caused me to drink an overabundance of water.

I came out of the bathroom and climbed back into bed.

The hall door opened silently, and the reddish-haired nurse came in.

17

She was wheeling a medicine cart in front of her, a cart covered with a chaos of bottles and vials and hypodermic needles. Having gotten the job as my regular full-time nurse seemed to have given her self-confidence. And she smiled at me brilliantly and introduced herself.

"I'm Miss Nolton, Mr. Rainstar. Full name, Kate Nolton, but I prefer to be called Kay."

"Well, all right, Kay," I said, smiling stiffly (and doubtless foolishly). "It seems like a logical preference."

"What?" She frowned curiously. "I don't understand."

"I mean, it's reasonable to call you Kay since your name is Kate. But it wouldn't seem right to call you Kate if your name was Kay. I mean—oh, forget it," I said with a groan. "My God! Do you play tennis, Kay?"

"I love tennis! How about you?"

"Yeah, how about me?" I said.

"Well?"

"Not very," I said.

"I mean, do you play tennis?"

"No," I said.

She sort of smiled-frowned at me. She picked up my wrist and tested my pulse. "Very fast. I thought so," she said. "Turn over on your side, please."

She took a hypodermic needle from the sterilizer and began to draw liquid into it from a vial. Then she glanced at me, gestured with light impatience.

"I said to turn on your side, Mr. Rainstar."

"I am on my side."

"I mean the other side! Turn your back to me."

"But that wouldn't be polite."

"Mr. Rainstar!" She almost stamped her foot. "If you don't turn your back to me, right this minute. . . !"

I turned, as requested. She jerked the string on my pajamas and started to lower them.

"Wait a minute!" I said. "What are you doing, anyway?"

She told me what she was doing, adding that I was the silliest man she had ever seen in her life. I told her I couldn't allow it. It was the complete reversal of the normal order of things.

"A girl doesn't take a *man's* pants down," I said. "Everyone knows that. The correct procedure is for the man to take the *girl's—ooowtch!* WHAT THE GODDAM HELL ARE YOU TRYING TO DO, WOMAN?"

"Shh, hush! The very idea making all that fuss over a teensy little hypo! Sergeant Claggett told me you were just a big old baby."

"That's why he's only a sergeant," I said. "An upper-echelon officer would have instructed you in the proper treatment of wounds, namely to kiss them and make them well."

That got her. Her face turned as red as her hair. "Why you . . . you . . . ! Are you suggesting that I kiss your *a* double *s*?"

I yawned prodigiously. "That's exactly what I'm suggesting," I said, and yawned again. "I might add that it's probably the best *o* double *f* offer you'll ever get in your career as an assassin."

"All right," she said. "I think I'll just take you up on it. Just push it up here where I can get at it good, and—"

"Get away from me, goddammit!" I said. "Go scrub out a bedpan or something."

"Let's see now. Ahh, there it is! *Kitchy-coo!*"

"Get! Go away, you crazy broad!"

"*Kitchy-kitchy-coo. . . .*"

"Dammit, if you don't get away from me, I'm going to . . . going to . . . going—"

My eyes snapped shut. I drifted into sleep. Or, rather, half sleep.

I was asleep but aware that she had dropped into a chair, that she was shaking silently, hugging herself, then rocking back and forth helplessly and shrieking with laughter. I was aware when other people came into the room to investigate—other nurses and some orderlies and a couple of doctors.

The silly bastards were practically packed into my room. A couple of them even sat down on my bed, jouncing me up and down on it as they laughed.

I thought, *Now, dammit*—

My thought ended there.

I lost all awareness.

And I fell into deep, unknowing sleep.

I slept so soundly that I felt hung over and somewhat grouchy the next morning when Kay Nolton awakened me. She looked positively aseptic, all bright-eyed and clean-scrubbed. It depressed me to see anyone look that good in early morning, and it was particularly depressing in view of the way I looked, which, I'm sure, was ghastly. Or shitty, to use the polite term.

Kay secured the usual matchbook-size bar of hospital

soap—one wholly adequate for lathering the ass of a sick gnat. She secured a tiny wedge of threadbare washcloth, suitable for scrubbing the aforementioned. She dumped soap and washcloth into one of those shiny hospital basins—which, I suspect, are used for puking in as well as sponge bathing—and she carried it into the bathroom to fill with water.

I jumped out of bed, flattened myself against the wall at one side of the bathroom door. When she came out, eyes fixed on the basin, I slipped into the bathroom and into the shower.

I heard her say, "Mr. Rainstar. *Mr. Rainstar!* Where in the world—"

Then I turned on the shower full, and I heard no more.

I came back into my room with a towel wrapped around me. Kay popped a thermometer into my mouth.

"Now why did you do that, anyway? I had everything all ready to—*Don't talk! You'll drop the thermometer!*—give you a sponge bath! You knew I did! So why in the world did you—*I said don't talk, Mr. Rainstar!* I know you probably don't feel well, and I appreciate your giving me a job. But is that any reason to—*Mr. Rainstar!*"

She relieved me of the thermometer at last, frowned slightly as she examined it, then shrugged, apparently finding its verdict acceptable. She checked my pulse, and ditto, ditto. She asked if I needed any help in dressing, and I said I didn't. She said I should just go ahead, then, and she would bring in my breakfast. And I said I would, and I did, and she did.

Since she was now officially my employee, rather than the hospital's, she brought coffee for herself on the breakfast tray and sat sipping it, chatting companionably, as I ate.

"You know what I'm going to do for you today, Mr. Rainstar? I mean, I will if you want me to."

"All I want you to do," I said, "is shoot me with a silver bullet. Only thus will my tortured heart be at rest."

"Oh?" she said blankly. "I was going to say that I'd wash and tint your hair for you. If you wanted me to, that is."

I grinned, then laughed out loud. Not at her, but myself. Because how could anyone have behaved as idiotically as I had? And with no real reason whatsoever. I had stepped on Jeff Claggett's toes, making a commitment without first consulting him. He hadn't liked that, naturally enough; I had already stretched his patience to the breaking point. So he had punished me—warned me against any further intrusions upon his authority—by expressing serious doubts about Kay Nolton. When I over-reacted to this, he had hastily backed-water, pointing out that he would not be leaving me in her care if he had had any reservations about her. But I was off and running by then, popping off every which way, carrying on like a damned nut, and getting wilder and wilder by the minute.

Kay was looking at me uncertainly, a lovely blush

spreading over her face and neck and down into her cleavage. So I stopped laughing and said she must pay no attention to me, since I, sad to say, was a complete jackass.

"I'm sorry as hell about last night. I don't know why I get that way, but if I do it again, give me an enema in the ear or something. Okay?"

"Now, you were perfectly all right, Mr. Rainstar," she said stoutly. "I was pretty far out of line myself. I knew you were a highly nervous type, but I teased you and made jokes when I should have—"

"When you should have given me that enema," I said. "How are you at ear enemas, anyway? The technique is practically the same as if you were doing it you-know-where. Just remember to start at the top instead of the bottom, and you'll have it made."

She had started giggling—rosy face glowing, eyes bright with mirth. I said I was giving her life tenure at the task of futzing with my hair. I said I would also give her a beating with a wet rope if she didn't start calling me Britt instead of Mr. Rainstar.

"Now that we have that settled," I said, "I want you to get up, back up, and bend over."

"B-bend over—*ah, ha, ha*—w-why, Britt?"

"So that I can climb on your shoulders, of course. I assume you are carrying me out of this joint piggy-back?"

She said, "Ooops!" and jumped up. "Be back in just a minute, Britt!"

She hurried out of the room, promptly hurrying back

164

with a wheelchair. It was a rule, it seemed, that all patients, ambulatory or not, had to be wheeled out of the hospital. So I climbed into the conveyance, and Kay fastened the crossbar across my lap, locking me into it. Then she wheeled me down to and into the elevator and subsequently out of the elevator and into the lobby.

She parked me there at a point near the admitting desk, admitting also being the place where departing patients were checked out. While she crossed to the desk and conferred with the registrar—or *un*registrar —I sat gazing out through the building's main entrance, musing that the hospital's charges could be reduced to a level the average patient could pay if so much money had not been spent on inexcusable nonsense.

A particularly execrable example of such nonsense was this so-called main entrance of the hospital, which was not so much an entrance—main or otherwise—as it was a purely decorative and downright silly part of the structure's facade.

The interior consisted of four double doors, electronically activated. The exterior approach was via some thirty steep steps, each some forty feet in length, mounting to a gin-mill Gothic quadruple archway. (It looked like a series of half horseshoes doing a daisy chain.)

Hardly anyone used this multimillion-dollar monstrosity for entrance or egress. How the hell could they? People came and went by the completely plain, but absolutely utilitarian, side-entrance, which was flush with the abutting pavement and required neither stepping down from nor up to.

It was actually the only one the hospital needed. The other was not only extravagantly impractical, it also had a kind of vertigo-ish, acrophobic quality.

Staring out on its stupidly expensive expanse, one became a little dizzy, struck with the notion that one was being swept forward at a smoothly imperceptible, but swiftly increasing, speed. Even I, a levelheaded, unflappable guy like me, was beginning to feel that way.

I rubbed my eyes, looked away from the entrance toward Kay. But neither she nor the admitting desk were where I had left them. The desk was far, far behind me, and so was Kay. She was sprinting toward me as fast as her lovely, long legs could carry her, and yet she was receding, like a character in one of those old-timey silent movies.

I waved to her, exaggeratedly mouthing the words "What gives?"

She responded with a wild waving and flapping of both her arms, simultaneously up and down as though taken by a fit of hysterics.

Ah-ha! I thought shrewdly. Something exceeding strange is going on here!

There was a loud SWOOSH as one of the double doors launched open.

There was a loud "YIKE!" as I shot through it.

There were mingled moans and groans, yells and screams (also from me), as I sped across the terrazzo esplanade to the dizzying brink of those steep, seemingly endless stone steps.

I had the feeling that those steps were much higher than they looked and that they were even harder than they looked.

I had the feeling that I had no feeling.

Then I shot over the brink and went down the steps with the sound of a stuttering, off-key cannon—or a very large frog with laryngitis: *BONK-BLONK-BRONK*. And I rode the chair and the chair rode me, by turns.

About halfway down, one of the steps reared up, turned its sharp edge up, and whacked me unconscious. So only God knows whether I or the chair did the riding from then on.

And We in Dreams

H. R. F. KEATING

H. R. F. Keating is the creator of Inspector Ghote of Bombay. His first Ghote novel, The Perfect Murder *(1964), received the Gold Dagger of the British Crime Writers Association and the Edgar Allan Poe Award from the Mystery Writers of America; and* The Murder of the Maharajah *(1980) won his second Gold Dagger. He also received a special Edgar for his nonfiction work* Sherlock Holmes, The Man and His World. *"And We in Dreams" first appeared in* Winter's Crimes 15; *this is the first publication in America. Mr. Keating, who reviewed crime fiction for the* Times *(London) for 15 years, lives in London.*

THOMAS HENNIKER nearly told his wife about the first dream as soon as he woke up. But then he didn't.

Yet it had been so extraordinarily vivid that it had been only a last-second decision that had stopped him turning to his Mousie, Mousie lying on her back beside him as always, stiff and tall as a soldier, and, breaking the constraints of a lifetime, tapping her on the shoulder and telling her in full detail everything that had happened to him in the sleep world.

Thank goodness, he thought as he lay waiting for the alarm to go off. Thank goodness, I didn't.

What would Mousie have thought, have said, if he had told her that, even in dream, he had coolly and deliberately begun to rob the firm? Thomas Henniker, with thirty-five years' unswerving service to Maggesson's Mail Order, systematically robbing them? Thomas, who as a boy had never so much as taken a sweet from the tin without permission, to have begun abstracting a huge sum from the firm that had been his employer all his working days.

Even now, he realised, he still had a small urge to say out loud the dreadful thing he had been doing. It was all so clear. Every detail was still vividly with him. Perhaps only speaking of it, thrusting it all into the clear light of day, would get rid of it, would make it vanish like a twist of fog as the rare dreams he ever had did at the shrill sound of the alarm on the table beside him.

The clock, rattling off as it always did at the exact stroke of 7:30, removed this last temptation.

Thomas swung back the bedclothes and set his little feet on the chilly floor.

But the regular bustle of his morning routine did not chase away the awful thing he had been doing in the secret hours of the night, the thing that the real Thomas Henniker, carefully shaving his red, round, chubby cheeks in front of the bathroom mirror, would never have done. Could never have done. Could never,

never, never do. Still, as he brought the safety-razor smoothly down towards his chin, he could see himself sitting operating the very computer which it was his duty from time to time to work at and obeying that extraordinary voice that had seemed to come out of the console itself. Obeying the wicked instructions of that awful, wheezy, rhythmical voice, like a mouth-organ articulating, as it told him how to put money into the Zygo account.

Zygo. That name. That extraordinary name. How could he, even in sleep, have come to think it? The name that was bound to come at the very end of the series of sales-commission accounts so that, by a process he was unable to understand, it was easy to direct sums into it from hundreds of other accounts scattered up and down the country. To direct into this convenient, accessible slot all those tiny, unregarded decimal points of cash that no one was going to query. How could he have invented all that? And then the diabolical final twist. He could remember it as clearly as all the rest. The way in which you instructed the machine to take all the decimal pence that followed the memorable pounds, except for those numbering less than 10. Then no one would eventually be alerted by the fact that their account always seemed to come to an exact figure.

It was really extraordinarily clever.

Thomas Henniker nicked himself with the razor. It was something he had not done for five years at least. Probably ten.

"Thomas," Mousie said the moment he presented himself for breakfast. "You've given yourself a cut.

There, just at the point of your chin. How could you be so careless? Today of all days."

What was today? Why was it "of all days"? For a moment his mind, where usually all the facts of his existence stood neatly tabulated, topsy-turvied in uncertainty. Then he remembered. This was the day that Mousie had fixed on for him to issue the dinner invitation to Mr. Watson, Mr. Watson, a good ten years his junior, who had swept effortlessly to a seat on the board and the managership of the department in which he himself had year by year climbed at last to the assistant managership. To Mr. Watson and Mrs. Watson, Mrs. Watson who was rumoured among the junior staff to be an Honourable.

It had been a task he had tried to wriggle out of. But Mousie had been adamant.

"It's no use your just being good at your work, Thomas. If you're going to get promotion before it's too late, you've got to show you're made of the right stuff. You've got to show you possess *savoir-faire*."

The brimming *r*s of her Aberdeen voice, granity like the pale grey, glittering stone of the far Northern city itself, had made a great deal of that last, scarifying French term.

And Thomas, deep within convinced he had not got *savoir-faire* and never could acquire it, had answered, firmly as he could, "Yes, dear."

So today he must make himself give the invitation, despite the unsightly little dab of cottonwool on his chin. Because if he did not, somehow, get that seat on the board he would never be able to provide his Mousie at the closing of her days with the house in the Dee Valley on which she had set her heart, a house standing in its own grounds somewhere in that infinitely desirable area presided over by Balmoral Castle itself, Scottish home of Her Majesty.

And now, seated opposite him at the little table, teapot in its embroidered cosy in front of her, Mousie began to let forth a curious keening sound.

He had half-known it was bound to come at this moment, and had inwardly dreaded it. She was embarking on her favourite poem, the only poem either of them had ever spoken aloud in all the thirty years of their life together, the Canadian Boat Song.

"From the lone shieling of the misty island
Mountains divide us, and the waste of seas—
Yet still the blood is strong, the heart is Highland,
And we in dreams behold the Hebrides!"

The first time she had voiced this yearning, in the same dirgelike tones she used now, Thomas had been foolhardy enough to point out that, though Deeside did indeed fall just within the Highlands, the Hebrides were in fact on the very other side of Scotland. He had not come top in geography at school for nothing.

But he had long ago learnt that when his Mousie keened out these words in this manner they merited only the tribute of silence.

And now that tribute earned him an unexpected reward.

"Perhaps, Thomas," his wife said, lifting the teapot, "you had better leave asking the Watsons till tomorrow. I don't know what he might think of you, going up to him looking like that."

"Yes, Mousie," Thomas said.

And off he went to work, not a minute late, not a minute early. He never was. But when in the course of his duties he had to enter some information on the computer a tiny sweat broke out all along the top of his chubby shoulders as he sat down at the console. He could remember exactly what that wheezing, rhythmical, mouth-organ voice had instructed him to do.

Later, over his solitary lunch, he thought about it. Somehow, he reasoned, he must have acquired the information necessary to carry out that appalling scheme without having realised it. When he had first been shown how to use the computer he had not bothered himself with anything more than he would need to know to give it such new instructions as might from time to time be required. If he had been told any of the theory behind the practicalities he had ignored it. Or so he had thought. But perhaps some of it had stuck. And then, too, he had always been good at figures. He could remember his father, when he was no more than eight or nine, saying, after they had been playing some arithmetic game as the three of them had sat at Sunday dinner, "Mother, that boy's got a real head for figures. He's going to go far one of these days." It had been one of the proudest moments of his life.

But he had never thought it would lead him to this.

To this terrible knowledge that he seemed to have acquired from nowhere.

For all the rest of that day he forced himself to concentrate ferociously on his work. And at home in the evening there was luckily a good documentary on television which helped keep his mind off the awful thought and when that was over they watched the news as usual and then set about their customary evening chores getting to bed exactly at eleven as they always did.

But no sooner had he put out the bedside light and settled down on his pillow than the voice that had wheezed and commanded in his sleep the night before came back into his mind exactly as he had heard it. It was like a belch recalling the flavour of a meal eaten hours earlier. And it left an equally sour feeling in his stomach.

Surely he was not going to dream that dream again? It took him a great deal longer than usual to get to sleep. Each time he had felt himself dropping off the voice he had thrust out of his mind began sounding there again and he had had to force himself into wakefulness to dispel it.

Yet at last he did get off. Only to be woken by the clatter of the alarm with all that sequence of events doubly clear in his head. In sleep the voice had led him along the same path again, in every appalling detail.

He did not cut himself shaving. But at breakfast he found himself putting a strange proposition to his Mousie.

"Dear, I've been thinking," he said.

He had not. He had not had the faintest notion of what he was about to say until he had begun to speak.

"Dear, I've been thinking. Perhaps when it comes to our holiday we ought to give Bournemouth a miss this year and instead . . ."

He paused. It was a monstrous idea that had come to him.

"Well, what about us taking a trip up to Scotland? To Deeside? We could look at some properties. Spy out the lie of the land."

Mousie's granite face broke into one of its rare smiles. It was as if the sun had glinted out in her native Aberdeen and the grey old buildings had suddenly sparkled with a hundred thousand little points of light.

"Oh, Thomas," she said.

The rest of breakfast passed without her mentioning that, undabbed by cottonwool now, he ought to invite the Watsons. And she did not even telephone during the course of the day, though she was always a great one for ringing with little reminders. It was something that deeply embarrassed him, though he had never spoken of it.

But his day was not happy. Every time he had occasion to use the computer the thought of that twice repeated dream came crowding back to him. And with it came the sombre realization that he had actually begun, as if he were delicately dipping a toe into cold water, to consider the possibility of carrying out the plan. Why else, he asked himself, had he made that suggestion to Mousie? At his present salary and with his actual prospects he would never be able to afford the sort of house Mousie wanted in the area he had proposed going to. What had entered into him? What was happening?

That night as he dropped his head on to his pillow he was not in the least surprised to find himself recalling the voice of the tempter. He almost welcomed it, and fell asleep as quickly as ever he had.

And dreamt the dream once more, heard once again that curious name Zygo, was instructed in the way this last place in the computer's series could be used for his gain.

Buffeted to and fro in the crowded tube train on his way to the office next morning, he somehow found that he had decided that he was going to set up the Zygo operation. Of course, he told himself, there was no question of opening a bank account in the name of a non-existent commission agent called Zygo so as to draw out any actual cash. He was just going to see if the whole complex routine he now knew so well worked.

Perhaps it wouldn't. Perhaps it was "all a dream." And, even if he did succeed in transferring all those few, scarcely wanted pennies into the Zygo slot, well, without a bank to put the money into he would not truly have stolen anything.

It worked all right. Just before the end of the day he requested from the computer, to which he had devoted a quiet half-hour almost as soon as he had got in, the figure for the balance in the last place in the sales-commission series. And up it came. A hundred and fifty-seven pounds, forty pence. It was no fortune. But it had shown that the scheme worked. And, unless at the first opportunity he undid that careful half-hour's work of the morning, with each day that passed a similar sum would accrue to the Zygo account.

On his way home, walking from the station, Thomas Henniker found he was calculating how many working-days would be needed to put into the Zygo account an amount large enough to acquire for his Mousie her dream house. He worked out that, as it so happened, the period would take him neatly to the date at the end of the following year when he could take an early retirement.

It was a very different situation from wondering, as he had been accustomed to do, whether the firm would allow him to soldier on past the usual retirement age in the hope, probably vain, that in that way he might accumulate enough at last to buy some sort of a house just outside Aberdeen.

He gave himself a little shake. Of course, there could be no question of an early retirement.

But, when he reached home and Mousie began at once to talk about their Deeside holiday, he came out, chirpy as a parrot, with a broad hint that his investments, in reality pitifully small and painfully cautious, had been doing surprisingly well and that an early retirement was something they might well be thinking about.

Mousie made no further reference to entertaining the Watsons either that evening or in the days that followed. And at night Thomas did not in his sleep hear again the wheezing, insistent voice.

He did not need to. He had begun to accumulate his retirement fund. Somehow he had crossed his Rubicon while he was, so to speak, looking over his shoulder at the distant view. Only occasionally, as the weeks went by, did he find it necessary to comfort himself with the thought that he had not yet opened a bank account in the name of Zygo and that theoretically Maggesson's Mail Order had not yet been robbed.

September came, and with it his holiday. (He always took this late since he felt it only fair to let members of the staff with children, though junior to him, have July and August.) Up and down the length of Deeside he and Mousie roamed, looking at every house on the market.

In the end they found a place that seemed ideal. It had been empty for a good while and they were told there was no hurry to put down the fairly large deposit required.

That night in bed Mousie recited her verse of the Canadian Boat Song, but with a triumphant rather than a keening note in her voice. First thing next morning Thomas slipped away "for a walk" and drew out a good sum from his own bank account and in a different bank opened an account in the name of John Zygo. He thought, as he signed the necessary forms, that John sounded a good honest forename.

Back at work, at the very first opportunity he requested from the computer the balance in the last in the series of sales-commission accounts. He had not made such a request after his first confirmatory one, but now he wanted to know just how much there was in the Zygo account that by writing one single cheque he could get into his hands. He imagined that, in fact, it would be about a quarter of the total needed for the house, quite enough to cover the deposit.

In moments the figure he wanted appeared.

He looked at it in astonishment, blinked, looked again, felt an overwhelming sense of puzzlement blossom in his head like a cloud of exploding dust.

The figure was only three hundred and twenty-four pounds, twenty pence.

It could not be right. Feverishly, with sweat-slippery fingers, he requested the information again. And got the same answer. Had the computer made a mistake? But computers never make mistakes. There is only human error.

He found it so difficult to concentrate when he got back to his desk that, after two more vain visits to the computer console, he went to Mr. Watson and said he felt indisposed and wanted to go home.

Walking slowly to the tube and on the train and walking slowly from the station, Thomas battered at his brain to seek some explanation of what had gone wrong. He could think of nothing. He had faithfully carried out the directions the mouth-organ voice had given him in those three successive dreams. He could not have forgotten a single detail. He was not accustomed to making mistakes. Never in all the years he had been with the firm, even when he had just been a youngster, had anyone ever found an error in his work.

But now something had gone wrong, wildly wrong. And he could not, could not, think what it was.

He sat miserably all that evening, puzzling and puzzling. But he had so little knowledge of computer theory, beyond that which he had so mysteriously acquired, that he could think of no conceivable explanation. Mousie, who had been astonished at his early return, and disappointed, began at last to express concern. She talked of telephoning the doctor, but he dissuaded her. At last he agreed to take a small hot toddy and go early to bed.

On the way upstairs, still puzzling, still acutely miserable, an idea came to him. Perhaps already the heated fumes of his little tot of whisky had penetrated his brain.

Could he possibly get in contact again with that voice inside the computer console? Could he dream that dream once more? Then, surely, the answer to this terrible snag would be given him. Then he could resume operations, take out of the Zygo account the sum necessary for the deposit on Mousie's dream house and be back on the rosy path once more.

Hastily he got into his pyjamas, turned down the bedspread and slid beneath the covers. He flung his chubby head on to the pillow passionately as any lover and sought to bring back to his memory the exact tones of that wonderful, wheezy, commanding voice.

He felt he had got it straight away. On those three miraculous nights months earlier it had made such an impression on him that he could not forget it.

But, though he was sure he was recalling the voice perfectly correctly, sleep did not come. His mind tossed and jumbled excitedly and he stayed blindingly awake.

An hour later when Mousie came up he was still wide-eyed. She advised aspirin and he swallowed down two tablets gratefully. Surely they would make him go to sleep.

They did, eventually. But he did not dream. Or if he did, the shrilling of the alarm clock in the morning dispersed his visions as completely as it had done in the days before he had dreamt the Dreams.

He went into work, and by taking a firm hold of himself managed to get through the day. He made no further attempts to ascertain the balance in the last in the series of sales-commission accounts. He knew that he would only get the answer he had got each time the day before, that ridiculous three hundred and twenty-four pounds, twenty pence.

Back at home, he began to put into operation a carefully thought-out programme designed to make himself sleep like a log. He went out into the garden and did some vigorous, but quite unnecessary, digging. He ate more than he usually did, but took the greatest care to chew everything even more thoroughly than was his custom so as to avoid the least possibility of indigestion. He asked Mousie to make him a hot drink last thing.

When he got to bed he fell asleep almost before he had brought to his conscious mind once more the authoritative, mouth-organ tones. But in dream-land he never got anywhere near his familiar computer console.

Night after night now he tried the same routine. The vegetable beds at the bottom of the garden became so well tilled they resembled a row of little sandy beaches. Mousie expressed anxiety about him getting fat as he chewed his way through heavy meal after heavy meal. And she had to buy a new tin of Ovaltine a whole fortnight earlier than usual. But night after night Thomas was unable to persuade the voice he so easily conjured up while still awake to stay with him in sleep.

Soon from constant worry, despite his hearty evening meals, he began to lose weight and at last Mousie ordered him off to the doctor. There, with a cunning he had not known he possessed, he told a tale about sleeplessness and was rewarded with a supply of pills. But even their narcotic effect could not get him back to that distant, tantalising place where the answer to his problem lay.

Each single night that haven, once visited on three successive occasions with such ease, defied his best efforts to reach it. And after a little Mousie began to take his new haggard look for granted. She ceased plaguing him about his health and began instead to plague him about her future.

Why had he not put down the deposit on the house on Deeside, she asked. It was bound to be snapped up. It was such a desirable property. He managed to produce excuses. Wrapping things up as much as he could in financial jargon, he made out that this was a particularly bad time to realise investments. If they waited just a little longer they would have a great deal more for the eventual purchase price.

But he was not able to put her off for long, and when she returned to the subject she had remembered in detail all his arguments and questioned him sharply about whether the situation had got better. He had a hard time proving to her that it had not.

Next day on the way back from the office a desperate expedient occurred to him. He stopped at an off-licence and bought a bottle of whisky. He sneaked it into the house under his raincoat and in the privacy of the lavatory at odd moments took swigs from it in an effort to get drunk, a state he had never been in before during the whole of his life.

By bedtime the bottle was still more than half full and, though he felt swimmy, he knew himself not to be as removed into another state as he believed he needed to be. He made one final visit to the lavatory, ignoring Mousie's asking whether he was "upset," and there manfully swallowed down a whole third of the bottle of stinging stuff. He sat there for a little afterwards and when he got to his feet realised that at last he was well and truly affected. Holding hard to the bannister he made his way upstairs. But he had hardly got half way when sudden nausea overwhelmed him and he had to go helter-skelter down again to be comprehensively sick.

Wan and washed out, he toiled his way to bed. But it was all he could do once his head was safely on the pillow to recite inwardly the briefest of wheezed-out litanies.

He woke next morning with a sharp headache and not the least recollection of any instructions received in the sleep-sodden hours.

Next weekend, when Mousie again asked him about

his investments and keened out once more, as she did most days now, that her heart was Highland, he quarrelled with her.

He was unable to get to sleep till past 2 A.M. that night, and lay cursing himself for the dream-hours being uselessly wasted.

When he did get off, he dreamt that he was in the office. But he was nowhere near the computer. Instead Mr. Watson was inviting him to meet his wife but telling him he could not possibly do so in the clothes he was wearing. He looked down at himself. He was naked.

He woke before the alarm clanged out. He was sweating. And he felt more tantalised than ever.

Three days afterwards he told Mousie he did not think the purchase of a house as old as the one in the Dee Valley was wise. He brought out a whole string of facts, and some fancies, about dry rot, drainage, roof repairs and landslip. She listened to him in grim silence.

Without another word being spoken that night they retired to bed and Thomas forgot, for the first time since his trouble had begun, to bring to his conscious mind the rhythmic sound of the mouth-organ voice.

And in the night it told him what had gone wrong. The dream came back, and with it the answer. It was laughably simple. Almost as soon as he had invented the Zygo slot a new agent had been taken on somewhere by the firm with a name that happened to begin with letters further on in the alphabet than Zygo.

The voice had gone on to wheeze out at him the necessary instructions for overcoming this absurd hold-up. All that he had to do was to open another account under a name with letters yet later than the newcomer's and then transfer the sum in the Zygo account to this fresh one.

He woke with everything once more magically clear in his head.

For a little while the problem of finding what letters would be sufficiently late to make sure of obtaining that last place in the computer series worried him. Until now he would have bet, only he had never been a betting man, that Zygo was as far along as anyone could get. But in the jostle of the tube a solution occurred to him. He felt a little jounce of pride. Here was something he had worked out entirely by himself, without the least prompting from the wheezy, commanding voice. And it was ingenious, most ingenious.

As soon as he got to his desk he took an internal memorandum form and boldly addressed it to the Chairman of the company. In it he suggested that a good advertising campaign might be run on the lines of *We cater for everybody from A to Z* and that the names of the agents who at present headed and ended their whole roll might be quoted.

He waited, patiently as he could, for a reply. That night he did not dream again that he was at the computer console. But he took this as a good sign. He had been told all that he needed to know and he was doing what he had been instructed to do. All was well.

It was, too. Next day he received an internal memorandum initialled by the Chairman himself. It warmly welcomed his suggestion. Thomas felt that, if he had still been concerned about a seat on the board, he would have taken a big step forward. Of course, the Chairman said, it would be necessary to obtain the permission of Mrs. Veronica Absolam and of Mr. Joseph Zzaman, "a new recruit, I find," to use their names, but this doubtless would be a formality.

So delighted was Thomas with this neat confirmation of how in the race to the end of the alphabet he had been, as it were, pipped at the post that immediately another bright idea came to him. One that could be put to the test at once.

He marched over to the corner of the main office where the London telephone directories were kept and turned to their very last page. And, yes, there was a name even later than Zzaman. It was Zzitz.

Well, Mr. Zzitz was going to acquire a brother. Who would open a sales-commission account with Maggesson's Mail Order this very day, and a bank account too. Mr. John Zzitz, was he that? No. No, he would be Mr. Adam Zzitz. The old Adam would rise up, and bring him luck.

He left the directories, put Mr. Adam Zzitz into the computer and then went to Mr. Watson's office and told him that he feared another of his "attacks" was coming on and he thought he had better go home. At the tube station he bought a ticket for the first remote suburb that came into his head and there opened the Zzitz bank account.

To avoid awkward questions from Mousie he spent the rest of the day in a cinema near the bank, seeing the film nearly twice over and not taking in a word of it. When he got back he gave Mousie his customary peck on her somewhat leathery cheek and told her without much preliminary that he had been talking on the phone to one of their Scottish agents and had managed to turn the conversation to the subject of house purchase. He had heard, he said, some rather good news.

"Places in Scotland in the days when our house was put up were built to last, you know. They're solid. Good foundations. Won't fall down like a house of cards."

He was rewarded with one of Mousie's granite-gleaming smiles.

At the office next morning he told Mr. Watson that he was quite recovered. "Never felt fitter really," he said cheerfully. "Never fitter in my life. And, you know, I think that's a good reason to take my retirement early. While I can still enjoy things. So I shall be going, not perhaps at the end of next year, but by the following midsummer. Yes, certainly by then."

Mr. Watson raised his eyebrows.

"Indeed? And—ahem—your pension, will it be adequate for all your needs, somewhat reduced as it will be?"

"I have some investments. In fact, I've been rather lucky with them, if I may say so."

Mr. Watson sighed.

Thomas, ending the conversation, went straight to the computer console. He sat down at it and began tapping the keys, if anything more businesslike and deliberate than usual.

Tap, tap, tap . . . The small balance in the new third-from-last Zygo account was transferred to the very end slot in the series and duly showed up there on request, three hundred and twenty-four pounds, twenty pence. Tap, tap. Tap, tap. Tap, tap . . . And the Zzitz account was ready to receive all the little unnoticed tail-ends from the accounts of every Maggesson agent and customer, sums that would amount to more or less a hundred and fifty pounds a day. By perhaps the following April they would total enough to cover the deposit on the Deeside house, a sum he had told Mousie, lying to her directly for almost the first time in all the years of their marriage, that had been paid already, but which the accommodating estate agent in Aberdeen had told him could be safely delayed for several months more. Then, quietly gobbling its little daily bites, the Adam Zzitz account would by the time his slightly postponed early retirement date came round have accumulated the whole purchase price of the place where Mousie's Highland heart could find rest at last.

His ten minutes' work at the console over, Thomas went back to his duties. He performed them with all his customary quiet efficiency.

And so he continued to do, past Christmas, noisily celebrated in the office, quietly celebrated at home, past the New Year—he first-footed the house carrying in his traditional Scots piece of shining black coal at two minutes past midnight, as he had always done—and into the Spring.

He decided towards the end of March that April the first would be a suitable day on which to complete the preliminary stage of the business. All Fools Day. He experienced at that moment a flowing jet of contempt for the whole hierarchy of Maggesson's Mail Order which simultaneously shocked and exhilarated him.

And on April the first just before noon, he went to the computer console and requested the total in the Zzitz account. He was not in the least surprised when this time, it amounted to a sum quite large enough to cover the deposit on the house. He tapped out certain further instructions, hardly having to think about what he was doing so embedded in his mind were the necessary sequences. Then, glancing round to make sure no other member of staff was within easy sight of his desk, he took from his briefcase his so far unused Adam Zzitz cheque book and made out a cheque payable to Thomas Henniker for the exact amount of the deposit on the house, safe in the checked and re-checked knowledge that already, thanks to the swiftness of electronic instruction, the credit would have gone from Maggesson's Mail Order to the imaginary Mr. Zzitz. Next from the briefcase he extracted two already stamped and addressed envelopes, one first-class directed to his bank, one second-class directed to the Aberdeen estate agents. He put the cheque for himself in the former, a cheque from himself in the latter and carefully sealed each one.

Then, although his lunch-hour was not for another fifty minutes, he got up from his desk and walked out of the building and round the corner to a post-box. He slipped the letters one by one into the appropriate slots.

It was done.

He turned and walked back towards the office, his steps a little slower now than their usual brisk trot.

Yes, he thought, finally I have gone past the place where there was any turning back. Yes, I am a criminal now. A criminal.

But he felt no shame.

Instead a feeling of high pride possessed him.

I am Man the hunter, he thought. I have provided for my mate. I have gone out and seized my prey. Yes.

At the entrance to the office young Mr. Francis, the firm's newest employee, was waiting for him. Hair appallingly long, of course, but nowadays what else could you expect?

"Telephone for you, Mr. Henniker. I believe it's Mrs. Henniker."

The boy wore a hint of an impudent smile. No doubt they had been gossiping to him already about Mousie's habit of phoning with little reminders.

"Very well, I'll take it directly."

He went to his desk and picked up the receiver.

"Yes, dear? It's me."

"Thomas, Thomas."

She sounded odd. Very odd. Shaken far out of her usual granite composure. Was she ill? She had, now he came to think of it, hardly uttered a single word at breakfast.

"Mousie, are you well?" he asked, totally forgetting to drop his voice as he said her name, a practice he had learned to adopt ever since he had once heard a giggle behind him.

"Yes, I'm well, Thomas. Perfectly well. But . . ."

"Yes? Yes? What is it? You don't sound at all—"

"Thomas, I had a dream last night."

"A dream? Did you say a dream? But you never dream."

"Thomas, I am telling you. I had a dream. A singular and horribly vivid dream. I dreamt I was warned by my poor dead mother in Aberdeen, solemnly warned, that if I ever set foot in Scotland again I should die. Thomas, I know that was a message. From beyond the grave. Thomas, we must not complete the purchase of the house. We must not, Thomas. Do you hear me?"

"Yes, dear," said Thomas Henniker.

A Bullet for Big Nick

MICHAEL AVALLONE

Michael Avallone, who calls himself "the fastest typewriter in the East," has published 207 novels and some 1,000 short stories or articles. He is perhaps best known for his Ed Noon private-eye novels. "A Bullet for Big Nick," Noon's first case, was written in 1949 but did not see print until 1958. Mr. Avallone lives in East Brunswick, New Jersey, surrounded by his movie, baseball, and detective-story collections.

A GOOD COP was dead. I had to do something about it. So I went down that night to see Big Nick Torrento at the Blue Grotto club. If a bigshot hood has no use for policemen, he has absolutely no time for private detectives.

Velvet, one of Nick's hand maidens, with blue chin and gun to match, made that pretty obvious at the door leading to Torrento's *sanctum sanctorum*. I didn't stop to talk. I hit him with all the hate I had in me. I wasn't thinking very straight. I had spent a terrible five minutes at the police morgue trying to recognize what was left of my friend, Mike Peters. I might never be able to eat hamburger again.

I was inside Big Nick's office, locking the door behind me fast, and digging out my .45. I wanted to be alone with the man I was sure had ordered the murder of Mike Peters.

"Hey! Who let you in here without knocking?"

Big Nick Torrento was staring at me curiously from the depths of a large, square desk. The marble inlaid top gleamed. His black eyes popped, then narrowed shrewdly.

"What kinda amateur show is this, Eddie? I got enough entertainment for the club right now."

Torrento didn't scare easy. He was Big Nick, owner of his own night club and a mob ruler on the same plane with the Capones and the Anastasias of old. His small, black eyes glittered with contempt for me. The simple fact that he had not raised his fat, ring-studded fingers was just another display of that contempt.

I moved slowly from the doorway, poking the .45, trying to keep a red haze out of my brain. "Evening, Nick. I came for a chat."

He grunted, rolling his cigar to the left side of his swab-lipped mouth. "How the hell did you get past Velvet? He never leaves my door. These monkeys of mine are getting careless."

"Velvet's all tied up right now," I said. "You've got a nice place here, Nick. Keeps your boys busy."

I could see he had reached the annoyance stage.

"You didn't come here to tell me what a nice dump I got. You better explain that hardware you're pushing in my face before I press a lot of buttons that'll get you a lot of bruises."

I didn't answer him directly. I jerked the slide of the .45, sending a shell into firing position. I had said plenty. Nick scowled, the angry furrows in his forehead deepening.

"C'mon, Ed. What's on your mind?"

I smiled. "Big Nick. That's you. Ed Noon. That's me. If Mike Peters was here, we could play a swell game of asking questions."

"What are you talking about, shamus?"

"I just came from the police morgue, Nick. You tell me. What's that poor kid now? Animal, vegetable, or mineral?"

"Oh, I get it now." Big Nick Torrento was smiling almost sympathetically at me. "Look, Ed. You can't pin that dead cop on this syndicate. We're legal. All through with the rough stuff." His tone was righteous and I had an uncontrollable urge to punch his face.

"Now that's funny. Velvet gave me the same argument out in the hall. But when he tried to back it up with brass knuckles, I gave him the back of my hand."

Nick Torrento puffed on his cigar.

"Okay. You and Mike Peters were friends. He was a swell guy and the department'll give him a swell funeral. Maybe a medal. But why blame me? If you hadn't quit the force six months ago for this private

eye stuff, you might have been with him on his last
job and it might not have happened."

That had been bothering me too.

"I might have been. But I wasn't and it did happen.
Which brings us right up to date, Nick. Me, with a
gun on your belly in your own little rat hole."

The office was large, soundproofed and plush. Just
the type the movies lead everyone to expect in the rear
of fancy night clubs run by gangsters. Only you never
got to see them unless you reneged on a bet or your
check bounced.

Big Nick leaned back in his chair, little eyes squint-
ing hard. "What have you got in mind, Ed? This can
cost you your license when I get in touch with my
mouthpiece. So you better make it good."

I showed him the nose of the .45. "You're on my
mind, Nick. You hold more appeal for me right now
than Elizabeth Taylor."

"Yeah? What does that mean?"

"Just this." I leaned across the desk. "When I can
pin this one on you, when I know for a fact that you
killed that kid, there's one in here with your name on
it." I tapped the barrel of the .45.

"You're crazy!" he roared.

"Am I? Mike Peters was working on your policy
set-up. Don't bother to deny it. He told me about it
three days before you stopped him."

Big Nick's beefy face paled, then reddened to nearly
match the heavy carmine drapes behind his chair that
blotted out the light of the alley.

"Listen, punk." He bounced to his feet angrily. "Nobody tells Big Nick what they're going to do. He tells them! The next move is mine, dummy." His big paw shot swiftly out of sight behind the desk. The hidden buttons routine.

I was glad he tried it. I chopped the .45 down in a vicious arc. The .45's barrel made a crunching noise that rang like music in my ears. Torrento shrieked like a woman and fell back into his chair. I followed him, coming around the desk and ramming the muzzle of the .45 into the base of his heavy chin.

"Feel it, Nick. Feel it. Like Mike Peters did when your boys worked him over with their blackjacks. Couldn't you give him a bullet, Nick? One quick slug? No, you had to pretty him up so they'd have a hard time identifying him. That was not nice, Nick, not nice at all."

Torrento strangled and swore. He tried to get out of the way but the gun pinned him to the chair. His black eyes were wide open now, in fear and bewilderment. His tongue lolled.

"Ed, whaddyaaaa—" he gagged. I reached down and dragged him to his feet. His bulk shivered. For one second, we stood eye to eye. Torrento, a fat, gasping hoodlum made rich by a world of suckers. Me, a poor man trying to tilt at a windmill. The only thing that separated our worlds and our intellects at this moment was the gun in my hand.

I hit him. His face dissolved in front of me in a blur of impact. The swivel chair squeaked noisily as his suddenly deposited bulk sat down again. His face twisted sightlessly toward the ceiling of his plush office.

I stared down at him. My forefinger tightened on the trigger of the .45. I had to shake my head to clear it of murder. Mike's bloody, battered face kept looking at me from the slab down at headquarters.

I heard the phone ringing suddenly. A jangling, jarring tingle of sound that brought me back to the present and where I was. Enemy territory.

It rang again. I scooped it to my ear, keeping an eye on the door, wondering how long it would take for Big Nick's cavalry to show up.

"Yeah?" I made my voice gruff and careless like Big Nick's. On a hunch.

"Nickie! I'm so glad you're in. It's me, Dolly. Nickie, I'm scared." It was a girl's voice, soft yet hard with fear. I thought fast. Dolly. Dolly Warren. The featured blues singer at the club. Nick's club, the Blue Grotto. The lovely face on the show case display outside.

"Keep talking," I said. "I'm busy."

"Oh, Nickie. I'm just getting ready to come down to the club for my number when I happen to look out the window and, Nickie, there's a man watchin' my place! I noticed him this mornin' too." She was wailing like a sick kid.

She was scared all right. I had heard fear before and she sounded like she had a solid dose.

"Stay put," I barked into the transmitter. "I'll send somebody over."

"Oh, Nickie." She was moaning again. "I'm scared."

"Shut up," I said.

"Do you think it has anything to do with that cop you had to get rid of?"

"You crazy canary, don't talk no more."

That's the way Big Nick would have shut her up. I never knew how I managed to keep the elation out of my voice. Right in my lap. She hadn't said it all but she had said enough. Later, I'd make her sing her head off in front of the police.

Dolly Warren started to mumble apologies but I cut her off. "Stay where you are. Be right over."

My fingers were trembling when I put the phone down. I holstered the .45 before I blasted Torrento right where he sat. Mike Peters' murder had hit me harder than I thought. But I needed more proof before I delivered the bullet to Big Nick.

I got out of the office, leaving him inert in the chair behind me. I carefully checked the long, low-ceilinged corridor. The hall was empty. The landing that led into the environs of the club showed no trouble.

Velvet was exactly where I had left him. Manacled to the railing, midway from Big Nick's private office. The strongarm man's eyes glared at me above the handkerchief wadded firmly in his jaws.

I retrieved the cuffs. Velvet tore at the gag and I let him have it again with the butt end of the .45. He collapsed without a whimper.

But my luck had changed. Coming over the landing on the dead run were a trio of shiny-haired men who must have spotted the scene from above. One quick look was enough. They were Big Nick's boys and loaded for bear.

I raced back the way I had come as a hoarse shout went up and gunfire ripped the confines of the corridor. I snapped a shot over my shoulder to discourage pursuit. It did. There was a mad scramble of dress suits for sections of safety.

There was a large frame window at the alley side of the end of the hall. I'd come in that way. It could serve as an exit, too. The alley was about six feet down.

I had one leg over the sill, ready to snap off another shot, when a noisy, searing poker buried itself somewhere in my left shoulder. The impact of the bullet sent me flying through the wide opening and I fell the rest of the way. The alley bottom crunched like conch shells beneath me. Knives of agony shot up my legs, reached the burning shoulder and the poker throbbed like a pneumatic drill. Behind me, more guns crashed.

I jerked another shot upward and lurched down the alley toward the street. Hugging the wall, I half ran, half dragged myself to my car.

I had finally stopped one. After years in the war and one police battle after the other, I had finally caught my bullet.

But all that was really unimportant; the only thing that counted was the bullet for Big Nick Torrento.

Dolly Warren was going to help me deliver that one.

She was gorgeous. Very gorgeous.

Milk skin, red mouth and dazzling blond hair that had to be her own. But she was stupid too. I could see it in the off-color eyes when she swung the door back and peered suspiciously at me over a span of chain lock.

"Who are you? What do you want? I don't know you."

"Nick sent me, Dolly. About that call and the party outside your window." I had to fight to keep the agony out of my voice. The shoulder had become a throbbing fire. The bullet had gone right on through without hitting a bone but it had cost me more blood than a handkerchief could stop.

"You must be a new one. Come on in. I got the creeps I guess." The door swung inward as she drew the chain with a clank of sound. She had been obviously drinking and was still too frightened to make the effort at thinking.

I followed her through a tiny hallway into one of the most expensively furnished apartments I'd ever been in on Central Park South. There were rich, deep rugs scattered all over the floor, fancy *objets d'art* cluttering every inch of the place. Nothing matched. The extreme decor of a built-in bar in the living room wasn't lost on me in spite of my condition.

Dolly Warren plumped down on a mountainous divan of fluffy cushions and poured herself a stiff drink from a chrome decanter. She looked at me as she swallowed her drink.

"Where's Nickie?" she snapped peevishly. "Why didn't he come? After all, I'm his girl."

I managed a weak smile. "Cops paid him a visit. Routine stuff. So Nick had to hang around to answer some questions. After all, he isn't running a civic center, lady."

She sneered and her beautiful face suddenly wasn't beautiful. "Funny man." A cloud shadowed her sneer. "You don't think their comin' had anythin' to do with —Say! What did you say your name was?"

I sat down with a short laugh, keeping my left side away from her so she couldn't see the stiff hang of the shoulder.

"Williams. Ted Williams. How about a drink, hon?"

I tapped the decanter so that it rang like a bell. She shrugged her bared shoulders and for the first time I was conscious of what she was wearing. A low-cut evening gown with a sash arrangement that accented her tigerish hips. I concluded it was the outfit she wore when she did her stuff at the Blue Grotto. She didn't have to sing in an outfit like that. I also concluded that she didn't know anything about baseball, the Washington Senators, or anything. The sky might be the limit, she was so stupid. Names meant nothing to her.

"I signed on with Nick last week," I explained as I might to a child. "I like a big operator. And Nick's plenty big enough for me. I go for a guy who's not afraid of the cops."

"Nick's not scared of anything." She nodded so hard her golden curls seemed to dance. "When one of those guys get too close, he swats them down like flies."

"Just like this Peters copper, huh?"

"Just like that—" She stiffened and for a moment a

flash of reasoning came into her blank light blue eyes. It was gone just as quickly. Her fright had come back.

"Never mind about that now. What about that guy beneath my window? Ain't you goin' to go down and see who he is?"

I shrugged my good shoulder at her. "What guy? Listen, I cased this place before coming in. If there was anybody hanging around before, he's gone now."

She flounced to the window and peered through dotted Swiss curtains. She whirled in disbelief. "He's gone! How do you like that? He's not there anymore." She clamped her hands to her forehead.

I remained where I was. "What's the matter, gorgeous?"

She wrung her red-tipped hands.

"Nick'll beat my brains out for draggin' him up here on a wild goose chase. But I swear there was somebody —oh, I need a drink."

She had two before she came up for air. I watched her with no expression on my face but a silly grin to hide the dull throb of the bad shoulder.

Dolly Warren was pretty drunk now but I let the drinks settle a while longer. I nursed my own drink getting as much good out of it as I could. It helped me forget the bullet hole.

"What's so funny?" She flung the question at me angrily.

"Just remembered a funny story a fellow told me the other day."

She brushed the curls out of her eyes. "Yeah? Well,

don't get funny. You're cute but I'm Nick's girl and he don't like nobody to get funny with me except him."

"Nick's a pretty funny guy himself."

"Ain't he though? Just like a big monkey." She ripped out a sudden throaty laugh. "You're sharp, Ted. Real sharp."

She fell back against the mountain of pillows with a seizure of laughter. Deep-chested, gutty, hard laughter. I knew it for what it was. She was getting hysterical.

I got up, reached her, and took her soft arm at the elbow. I squeezed the flesh gently. Sweat wasn't making me feel exactly cool but I shook the feeling off. Dolly Warren wasn't in any condition to notice.

"Nick's sharp too, Dolly. Nobody should ever cross Big Nick," I said.

That sobered her up a bit. "You said it. Wait'll you're around with him a little longer. You'll see."

"I don't have to be around long, Dolly. I read what happened to that cop Peters."

"Peters?" she simpered. "That's different. He was a cop and on Nick's back. He got too close to Nick's policy racket. So Nickie shut him up good." She made a cute expression with her face. I was grim, as she was singing her head off.

"I need a drink." I wasn't making conversation anymore.

"Where's Nickie?" She was impatient again, rubbing her elbow with one slender hand. She stood up, swaying. "Wait—we both need a refill. This waitin' drives you nuts, don't it?" She lurched over to the miniature bar and ducked behind its shiny back to rummage for something. Reappearing with a new bottle, she filled our glasses to the brim.

I arched my back to ease the deadness of my arm. I slid the .45 out of its harness and pointed it at Dolly Warren. She was bringing back the drinks with drunken alacrity when she saw the gun in my hand.

Flinging her hands to her face, she let the glasses crash to the floor. The flush of intoxication and her natural bloom of health drained right out of her curved cheeks.

"Sit down, sister."

She sat down without a murmur, her arms dangling without control, her soft body completely spent. Her vacant blue eyes got a shade darker.

"You're not from Nick," she moaned.

"No, I'm not."

"You're a cop!"

I shook my head. "No, Dolly. I'm the friend of a cop. A very dead cop. Mike Peters. Remember him, Dolly?"

"No!" It screamed out of her.

"He was a very good looking boy before he met up with those blackjacks."

Half mad with fright now, she sagged on the divan, one long, lovely leg trailing to the floor. She stared at me, her eyes wide pools of terror She was a child who had just found out the Sandman was real

"What are you going to do? I didn't have anything to do with it, I tell you."

I reached, grabbed a handful of her luxuriant curls and yanked her to a sitting position. She cried out with the pain of it and sat back gasping, her breasts heaving.

"Don't lie to me, Dolly. I want the whole rotten truth. Mike never would have gotten himself holed up in a dark alley like that unless a beautiful dish like you had arranged to meet him there. That was Mike's weakness. Beautiful dishes. But it's not mine."

She tried to clutch my gun hand in a burst of mad courage but I didn't let her. My open hard palm flicked twice. Two angry streaks of red flamed her cheeks.

"I want it now, Dolly. A full confession. It's that or this toy in my hand goes off. Know what a .45 would do to your face at this range?"

"Don't," she blubbered. "Not that. Honest, you got me all wrong. I never—"

She halted suddenly and the swift flash of relief that flooded her eyes made me freeze where I stood. I didn't turn or bat an eyelash. I'd forgotten about the front door. My burning shoulder and my blind anger had made me forget a lot of things.

"Don't move or you're a dead man," somebody behind me said in a voice that had no emotion at all. A door slammed shut violently and footsteps slithered in the foyer.

I spread my hands. The automatic fell to the rug. There wasn't anything else to do now. I waited. Dolly Warren rushed forward, crying.

"Get around, don't you, Eddie?" I didn't have to

turn around to know that Big Nick Torrento had put two and two together and come up with a fast, workable four.

They moved into the room from the fancy foyer. Big Nick Torrento, a battered looking Velvet and another hood whose face was new to me but his expression wasn't. They all had their hats on and the pair flanking Big Nick also had guns.

Torrento's face was a flabby mask of anger and Velvet was fairly licking his thin lips. The third man just kept his gun pointed at my head.

"Three to one, Nick? It hardly seems enough."

"Eddie, this was one hunch of mine that paid off. I was wondering what held Dolly up. Frisk him, Velvet."

Dolly was blubbering in Nick's arms. "Oh, Nickie, he hit me an' he was asking me all kinds of questions!"

They were all in front of me now and Nick was glaring. His face was livid. "Rough stuff, is that it? You're a little too free with your hands, Eddie. Go ahead, Velvet."

I knew what was coming but I couldn't get out of the way.

Velvet cackled and kneed me from behind. I doubled up and he came back with a bony fist that slammed me to the floor. I fell like a beat-up rug, the blood spinning in my head, red-hot rivets hammering away at the shoulder again. The floor swam in front of me. The point of something, it felt like Dolly Warren's high-heeled weapon, dug into my side. I tasted blood again.

"Hold it," Torrento's voice sounded above me.

"That's enough for now." Big Nick sounded far away. "Get some water, Dolly. I want to talk to him."

Water exploded in my face. I opened my eyes. I raised myself to one knee, holding back a groan. I tried a grin through my split lips.

"You boys don't really have to show me all this kindness," I muttered. Velvet's big hands helped me the rest of the way, shoving me roughly on to the divan.

Big Nick had one of his fat cigars going. His tiny eyes were shining with grudging admiration.

"You're tough, Eddie. I'll say that much for you. But I hate cops who get too close to me. Even ex-cops. Big Nick is paying for your last ride."

"I figured that, Nick."

Velvet suddenly looked surprised. "He's got lead in him now, boss. The boys did better than they thought."

"See, shamus?" Big Nick said. "Mess around us and you get hurt."

Blood and pain made me hold my teeth together. "Mike Peters got hurt too, Nick."

Torrento shook his thick head. "Got a one-track mind, you have. Yeah. Mike Peters. Your friend. He got close. Too close. So I pushed him out of the way. Dolly made that one easy. Once he caught her act, he was as good as dead."

I felt the blood pound in my skull. My left arm was useless now. Like I'd slept on it all night. Only bitter hate kept me going. Hate and the picture of Peters lying in an alley with his face all caved in. That and this lovely, stupid wench who had led him on with a kiss and a promise.

"I got news for you, Nick." It was my last card coming up. The only one left in a badly misplayed hand. "Mike died but he had his fun before he went."

Torrento grunted, his eyes narrowing. Velvet growled.

"What does that mean?"

"Dolly let him have some fun. Her own brand, the brand you know so well. Mike went out the way every red-blooded guy would like to go when they die. One last fling with a beautiful broad. You know what I mean."

I let that sink in, fighting to clear my head. Forcing a smile, I winked. That was too startling for their single-gauge intellects. Wounded, beaten men just don't wink and joke. Especially a man who is about to die.

Dolly Warren paled. The color left her face with the enormity of the lie.

Nick Torrento scowled. "Say it in English, Noon."

"Want me to use four-letter words in front of a lady? Mike and Dolly made love before he got killed—"

"Want Velvet to kiss you again, shamus?" Big Nick snarled. "Lay off that kind of talk! It won't buy you a thing!"

"That's just it, Nick. It won't. So I'm telling you for nothing. Go ahead. Ask her , urself."

Dolly Warren was no angel. But she was Nick Torrento's girl. Big Nick was shrugging his shoulders in contempt, willing to let it go at that, but not Dolly. Her meal ticket and her well-being were on the line.

She forced her way between the guns and glared down at me. Her blue eyes had tiny specks in them. Red specks of uncontrollable anger.

"You cheap, no-good excuse for a man! Sayin' things like that about me!" She moved in closer, her lithe body weaving in the evening gown. "I hope they cut out your rotten tongue. I want Nick to have your arms and legs pulled off, one by one! I want to see—"

It was what I had hoped for.

For split seconds she was between me and the guns in their hands. It was probably my last chance.

My foot came up with all the speed and force I could muster and everything I had left was wrapped up in it. With all the nerves and muscles in my body alive with pain, I rocketed her back the way she had come.

Dolly Warren's surprise and fright made windmills of her arms. She flailed wildly at Velvet and the third gun in the room. Her sudden weight sent them spinning backward, their guns falling. Big Nick started forward with a hoarse shout of warning, one fat hand clawing for a weapon. But the hand I had damaged in the office was slow. I had time to recover.

I rolled to the carpet, my fingers closing fast on Velvet's sleek-barreled .38. I came up with it, spitting fire and noise, feeling a mad wave of exultation surging over me.

Velvet had pulled another gun from his coat pocket

but not in time. He made a face as my slug thudded into his chest, then his mouth sagged and he crumpled like wet newspaper to the floor. His crony scrambled desperately for the cover of the built-in bar. He had another gun now too. I could see it was my own .45.

Big Nick had grabbed Dolly Warren. She squirmed in his arms as his meaning got home to her. They reeled in a curious dance of self-preservation as the hood behind the bar opened fire.

A slug tore a hole in the floor near my thigh. I maneuvered behind the divan. The lights of the room were changing like kaleidoscopes in front of me. I fought to keep my head and eyes clear. I was close to blackout.

I could hear Dolly Warren screaming and kicking to get free of her bear-like captor.

The hood behind the bar didn't see me prop myself on the arm of the divan, sight carefully and squeeze off three rounds. I raked the length of the bar. There was a strangled cry of surprise and a pair of trousered legs flopped into view from one corner of the thin-walled bar. I had estimated its solidity perfectly. The hood hadn't. He joined Velvet in oblivion.

My eyes swung back to Dolly Warren and Nick Torrento.

Toward their struggling, contrasting figures, Dolly, beautiful in her strapless, skin-tight gown. Big Nick, massive and dark in his full dress clothes. I cocked the gun, ready for the slightest opening. It never came.

The hall door was swinging inward again.

There were men in plainclothes, a flash of blue uniforms. I staggered erect as I spotted Lieutenant Drum. But they had come too late, also. For somebody.

There was a roar and a shot. Dolly Warren and Nick Torrento broke apart like dancers who have reached the end of the waltz. A gun thudded to the floor in the sudden stillness. Big Nick Torrento stared at Dolly Warren foolishly, then looked down at the widening red stain on his white shirt front. He giggled. A short, bubbly giggle. Dolly Warren moaned.

Nick Torrento crawled to the floor suddenly and curled up in a bulky heap at her feet.

The whites of Dolly Warren's eyes rolled up and her breath-taking figure sank down beside him. Then the shouting and movement started all over again. I heard Drum bellowing something.

That was all I saw because I fainted myself.

We were alone in Drum's office when the red-headed lieutenant of detectives let me have it with official scorn.

"You ex-cops are all alike! Think you can handle everything by yourselves. Why the hell didn't you tell our man Stone what you were up to? He'd been watching the dame's place since Peters got it. Did you think the department was asleep on the job?"

I lifted the clean white sling on my arm. "This was personal, Red. I thought you'd understand."

Drum's face got redder than his hair. "Sure, I understand. I've got some friends too. But this was a police case. And there are police methods, in spite of your peculiar ideas on the subject. You should have known better. We had Torrento in mind too. Peters had been assigned to his policy racket to get the evidence that would put him where he belongs."

I shook my head. "I wasn't counting on Big Nick having time to use a smart lawyer. This was the only way, Red. I'm sorry Dolly Warren beat me to it."

"Be glad she didn't miss." Drum pounded the desk. "I oughta grab your license for this. As a former cop you should have known better."

I stood up. He had iced me good and I didn't like it. "Is that all, lieutenant? My arm's starting to bother me."

Drum's freckled face broke into an exasperated smile. "Ah, get the hell out of here. I never could talk any sense into you. Go ahead. Be a private cop. Use a gun to win your argument. But don't expect any help from me."

At the door I turned. I owed him an explanation.

"Red, I know vendettas went out with gaslights but this was one time I couldn't turn the other cheek. If Big Nick was still alive, there'd still be a bullet for him. I don't give a damn about your feelings or the department's feelings, I'd still want to deliver it."

Drum said nothing but his expression had softened. He reached into his desk drawer and came up with a bottle with a bright label. He drew two shot glasses from a cabinet behind him.

"You intellectual gunmen make me sick," he said tiredly. "Come on back here, Ed. Let's drink a toast. To a swell cop. Mike Peters, your friend, *and mine*."

Trace of Spice

PETER LOVESY

Peter Lovesey is best known for his series of novels featuring the Victorian detective, Sergeant Cribb, who has been seen around the world on television. He prefers, he says, to regard his books as "Victorian police procedural novels." He was awarded the Gold Dagger of the British Crime Writers Association for The False Inspector Dew *(1982). Mr. Lovesey, a former college teacher who lives in Wiltshire, writes that he has made a living out of murder for ten years now. "Trace of Spice" is his most recent story.*

THE DETECTIVE-STORY WRITER, Lavinia Quan, blessed with a physique that was difficult to sidestep, had succeeded in stopping Justin Fletcher, who reviewed crime fiction for one of the Sunday papers. "Just the man I want a few words with," she told him ominously. "I wish to inform you that I have not altered my style of book in twenty years and I will not be bludgeoned into doing it by a newspaper critic."

"Bravely spoken," Fletcher tactfully remarked. "Why change a formula that pleases so many readers and brings you all those royalties?" Stupid old bat. Even if she turned her Inspector Fotherby into a compulsive flasher, it wouldn't salvage her books from their monumental tedium. "I hope my review last Sunday didn't upset you."

"Your phrase, Mr. Fletcher, was 'same old recipe without a trace of spice.'"

He coughed. Why the hell had she invited him to the party if the piece offended her? "Yes. The metaphor came over a trifle more strongly than I intended. But as a reviewer, Miss Quan, I'm bound to be sensitive to new trends in crime writing. Frankly, your world of country-house parties and decent-mannered detectives is somewhat outmoded."

"My stories have a foundation in fact, Mr. Fletcher, and so do my characters." The sweep of Miss Quan's glance took in most of the room.

God, yes! Why hadn't he seen it? This house of hers was the country mansion of all her novels. The people standing around were the stock set of suspects who inhabited it. He had already met half a dozen of them, and it had simply not dawned on him. There was the colonel by the french windows with the vicar. Under the chandelier was the eccentric professor making conversation with the inevitable doctor whose eyebrow twitched. The world of Miss Quan's books was still in existence, preserved like a pharaoh's tomb here in rural Sussex. There was even a butler—the butler who had done it nine times out of ten!—possibly on hire from a catering firm, but here to the life in tie and tails, carrying a tray of drinks.

Fletcher recovered himself. "Your characters, Miss Quan? Straight from life. It's your plots I find predictable."

She frowned. "Really? You attacked my last novel but one for being too implausible. Remember your words? I do. 'Miss Quan is welcome to select any murderer she likes from her cardboard-cutout kit of suspects. After twenty or more of her novels, I am indifferent to the latest arrangement. But I am bound to protest when she asks me to believe all fifteen of her suspects are equally guilty.' That was unkind, Mr. Fletcher. It spoiled the book for thousands who would have read it. I shall not forgive you for revealing the denouement of that book."

Fletcher bridled. He had taken enough of this. If she wanted the truth, she could have it. "The story was totally implausible. *Fifteen* people with grudges against one man, all combining to murder him? Pure fantasy. Any thriller writer deals in the bizarre and absurd to some extent, but a plot must have its thread of logic. Your book didn't. That's why I hammered it." He smiled. "Even so, I expect your loyal readers bought it in thousands."

"That isn't the point," said Miss Quan icily. Then, with an effort at sociability, "However, you'll have a drink? I didn't invite you here to have an argument."

"No argument," said Fletcher charitably. "Better if these matters are aired." He took a whisky from the butler's tray. There was a good selection of drinks, generous quantities ready poured in English cut glass. The old girl wasn't in penury yet for all the hostile reviews.

Miss Quan took a glass of Madeira and placed it on the mantelpiece nearby. "Implausible, you said. Suppose I told you, Mr. Fletcher, that I have devised another plot—a neater one, I believe—with the same result, that fifteen people are so united in hatred of one man that they combine to murder him?"

He laughed aloud. "*Julius Caesar*, eh? That wasn't a whodunit, as far as I recollect."

"No," said Miss Quan quietly. "I'm speaking of something more modern. Right up to date, in fact."

Fletcher was suddenly conscious that Miss Quan's voice was the only one in the room. All the other guests stood facing them, glasses in hand, listening.

She went on portentously, "If I told you that we are here tonight to participate in a murder, would you believe me, Mr. Fletcher? There are fifteen of us, if you include the butler, and he most certainly wishes to be included."

Fletcher's laugh had a note of unease. "What do you mean? Party games?"

"Not really. We invited you here to exact a kind of justice. You probably assumed that my guests were neighbors. Not so. The vicar there came up from his parish in Cornwall for tonight's party. You will know him better as Arnold Dellar, the author of *A Box for the Bishop*. Remember your review last October?"

The vicar himself recited it, intoning the words like the last rites: " '*Murder in the Cathedral*, modern style.

Plot rattles like a collection box. Enough padding to upholster all the pews in St. Paul's.' "

Nobody smiled.

"You were no less vitriolic toward the colonel over there," Miss Quan continued. *"The Bloody Brigadier* was his first crime novel and will be his last thanks to you. Yes, we are all crime writers who have suffered from your obnoxious brand of criticism—even the butler. Remember *Skulduggery in the Scullery?"*

Too well. Fletcher nodded, liking the situation less and less.

"I won't bore you by listing all the books you have destroyed in your column, Mr. Fletcher, although they meant a good deal to their authors. I shall return to an earlier point."

Thank God for that! Cold sweat was rolling down his sides.

"You dismissed the notion of fifteen people participating jointly in a murder as preposterous. Look around you, Mr. Fletcher. Do you doubt our ability to commit a crime? Aren't we the experts? And haven't we motive enough? When you have sacrificed countless precious hours to bring to life a work that a critic snuffs out in two sentences, you have the motive, believe me."

He was ready to believe anything.

"Since you are a connoisseur, Mr. Fletcher, I'll tell you how this plot unfolds. Each of us, naturally, is conversant with the properties of the deadly poisons. Instead of bringing bottles to the party tonight, my guests brought vials of strychnine, cyanide, digitalis, and others they could obtain. Everyone brought something—isn't that the rule at all the best modern parties? We added something deadly and quick-acting to each of the drinks on the butler's tray. You took a whisky, I notice, and you haven't tried it yet. I can't tell you what went into it, but we may know from your reaction. Aren't you going to try it?" Remembering something, Miss Quan snapped her fingers. "Of course! As a connoisseur, you want to know how we plan to dispose of the, em, inevitable. With a doctor and a vicar in our group, need I say more? Drink up, Mr. Fletcher."

He looked at the yellowy liquid. The idea was outrageous. Pure fantasy. A party joke. His gaze returned to the faces watching him, decent, inoffensive people anyone would respect. Would a doctor or a vicar countenance such a thing? It *had* to be an elaborate practical joke. The hell with them all.

He raised his glass high. "To crime, then, ladies and gentlemen," he announced, his confidence returning, "of the fictional kind!" Without another thought, he gulped it down and looked around the room.

No one else had lifted a glass.

Dead-End for Delia

WILLIAM CAMPBELL GAULT

William Campbell Gault has written some twenty-five crime novels since 1952, several of which feature Brock Callahan or Joe Puma. A veteran of the old Black Mask, *he has received an Edgar Allan Poe Award from the Mystery Writers of America and the 1984 Lifetime Achievement Award of the Private Eye Writers of America. "Dead-End for Delia" appeared in the November 1950 issue of* Black Mask Detective. *In the dedication copy of* The Blue Hammer, *Ross Macdonald wrote, "To Bill Gault, who knows that writing well is the best revenge." Mr. Gault lives in Santa Barbara, California.*

THE ONLY LIGHT in the alley came from the high, open windows of the faded dancehall bordering its east length. From these same windows the clean melody of a tenor sax cut through the murky air of the alley. There was nothing else around that was clean.

The warehouse running the west border of the alley was of grimy red brick, the alley itself littered with paper and trash, cans, and bottles. It was a dead-end alley, no longer used.

The beat officer was at its mouth, keeping the small crowd back, and now the police ambulance came from the west, its siren dying in a slow wail.

The beat officer said, "Better swing out and back in. Sergeant Kelley with you?"

"No. Why?" The driver was frowning.

"It's his wife," the beat officer said. "She really got worked over."

"Dead?"

"Just died, two minutes ago. How she lived that long is a wonder."

The driver shook his head, and swung out to back into the mouth of the alley.

From the west again, a red light swung back and forth, and the scream of a high speed siren pierced the night. The prowl car was making time. It cut over to the wrong side of the street and skidded for fifteen feet before stopping at the curb.

The man opposite the driver had the door open before the car came to rest, and he was approaching the beat patrolman while the driver killed the motor.

"Barnes? I'm Kelley. My wife—?"

"Dead, Sergeant. Two minutes ago."

Sergeant Kelley was a tall man with a thin, lined face and dark brown eyes. He stood there a moment, saying nothing, thinking of Delia, only half-hearing the trumpet that was now taking a ride at Dreamland, the Home of Name Bands.

Delia, who was only twenty-three to his thirty-seven, Delia who loved to dance, Delia of the fair hair and sharp tongue—was now dead. And that was her dirge, that trumpet taking a ride.

He shook his head and felt the trembling start in his hands. He took a step toward the other end of the alley, and the patrolman put a hand on his arm.

"Sergeant, I wouldn't. It's nothing to see. Unless you're a Homicide man, it's nothing you'd—Sergeant, don't."

Sergeant Kelley shook off the hand and continued down the alley.

Dick Callender of Homicide was talking to the M.E. He turned at the sound of Kelley's footsteps.

Dick said, "It's nothing to see, Pat."

Pat Kelley didn't answer him. There was enough light from the dancehall for him to see the bloody face of his wife and the matted hair above it. He hadn't seen her for four months.

Then he looked at Callender. "She say anything, Dick?"

"Just—*Tell Pat I'm sorry. Tell Pat Lois will know.* Make sense to you; the second sentence, I mean?"

"None," Pat lied. The band was playing a waltz, now.

Callender said, "We'll give it a lot of time. Homicide will shoot the works on this one."

Pat looked at him and used his title, now. "I want a transfer, Lieutenant. To Homicide." His voice was very quiet. "You can fix it."

A piece of dirty newspaper fluttered by, stirred by the night breeze. The white-coated men were laying the stretcher alongside the body.

Callender said, "We've got a lot of good men in Homicide, Pat." He didn't say, *And we want our suspects brought in alive.*

But Pat could guess he was thinking it. He said, "She left me, four months ago. I'm not going to go crazy on it, but I'd like the transfer."

"We'll see, Pat." The lieutenant put a hand on his shoulder. "Come on. I'll ride back to headquarters with you."

They went in the lieutenant's wagon. About halfway there, Pat said, "It could have been one of those—pick-up deals, some mugg out of nowhere who'll go back to where he came from." Shame burned in him, but he had to get the words out.

Callender didn't look at him. "I've got Adams and Prokowski checking the dancehall. They're hard workers, good men."

Pat said nothing.

Callender went on, quietly. "There must be some angle you've got on it. Your wife must have thought you knew this—this Lois, or she wouldn't have mentioned it. She didn't have enough words left to waste any of them on some trivial matter."

"My wife knew a lot of people I didn't," Pat said. "My statement will include everything I know, Lieutenant. Have her sent to the Boone Mortuary on

Seventh Street, will you? I'll talk to her mother to-night."

"She—was living with her mother, Pat?"

"No. I don't know where she's been living these past four months. But it wasn't with her mother. I wish to God it had been, now."

They made the rest of the trip in silence.

It was a little before midnight when Sergeant Pat Kelley, of the pawn shop and hotel detail, climbed the worn stairs of the four-story building on Vine. The place was quiet; these were working people and they got to bed early.

Mrs. Revolt lived on the third floor, in two rooms overlooking the littered back yard and the parking lot beyond. Pat knocked and waited.

There was the sound of a turning key, and then Mrs. Revolt opened the door. Her lined, weary face was composed, but her eyes quickened in sudden alarm at the sight of Pat.

"Pat, what is it?"

"I'd better come in," he said. "It's Delia, Mrs. Revolt. Something's happened. . . ."

She pulled her wrapper tightly around her, as though to stiffen her body against his words. "Come in, come in. But what—? Pat, she's not—it's not—"

He came into the dimly lighted room with the rumpled studio couch, the gate-leg table with the brass lamp, the worn wicker chairs, the faded, dull brown rug. In this room, Delia Revolt had grown from an infant to the beauty of the block. In this room, Papa

Revolt had died, and Pat had courted the Revolt miracle.

"Sit down, Mrs. Revolt," Pat said now.

She sat down in the wicker rocker. "She's dead, I know. She's dead. My Delia, oh Lord, she's dead." She rocked, then, back and forth, her eyes closed, her lips moving, no decipherable words coming out.

Pat sat on the wicker lounge. "She was found in an —she was found near the Dreamland dancehall. She's dead. There'll be detectives coming to see you; other detectives, Mrs. Revolt."

Her eyes opened, and she stopped rocking. "Murdered—Delia? It wasn't an accident? Murdered—Delia?"

He nodded. Her eyes closed again, and a strangled sound came from her tight throat, and she toppled sideways in the chair.

Pat got to her before she hit the floor. He put her on the studio couch, and was waiting with a glass of water when her eyes opened again.

Her voice was a whisper. "How did it happen?"

"She was hit with something blunt, concussion. Nobody knows anything else. But there's something I wanted you to know."

Fear in her eyes, now. She said nothing.

"Before she died, Delia mentioned a name. It was Lois. I told the officer in charge the name meant nothing to me. I told him I didn't know any Lois."

The frightened eyes moved around Pat's face. "Why did you say that?"

"Because they're going after this one. She's a cop's

wife and they won't be pulling any punches. This man in charge, Callender, can be awful rough. I'd rather talk to Lois, myself."

"But why should they bother Lois?"

"Delia mentioned the name, before she died. They're not going to overlook anything and they're not going to be polite."

"All right, Pat. I had a feeling, when you knocked, something had happened. I've had a feeling about Delia, for years. You can go now; I'll be all right. I'll want to be alone."

She was under control, now, this woman who'd met many a tragedy, who'd just met her biggest one. The fortitude born of the countless minor tragedies was carrying her through this one.

Pat went from there to Sycamore. He was off duty, and driving his own car. On Sycamore, near Seventh, he parked in front of an old, red brick apartment building.

In the small lobby, he pressed the button next to the card which read: *Miss Lois Weldon.*

Her voice sounded metallic through the wall speaker. "Who's there?"

"It's Pat, Lois. Something has happened."

He was at the door when it buzzed.

She was waiting in her lighted doorway when he got off the self-service elevator on the fourth floor. She was wearing a maroon flannel robe piped in white, and no make-up. Her dark, soft hair was piled high on her head.

Her voice was quiet. "What's happened?"

"Delia's been murdered."

She flinched and put one hand on the door frame for support. "Pat, when—how—?"

"Tonight. In the alley next to the Dreamland ballroom. Slugged to death. She didn't die right away. She mentioned your name before she died."

"My name? Come in, Pat." Her voice was shaky.

There wasn't much that could be done about the apartment's arrangement, but color and taste had done their best with its appearance. Pat sat on a love seat, near the pseudo-fireplace.

Lois stood. "Now, what did she say?"

Pat frowned. "She said, 'Tell Pat I'm sorry. Tell Pat Lois will know.' She told that to Lieutenant Callender of Homicide, before she died. He asked me who Lois was, and I told him I didn't know.'

"Why?"

"I was trying to protect you. It might have been dumb. But they're going to be rough in this case."

She sat down in a chair close by, staring at him. "I saw Delia two days ago, Thursday afternoon. She told me then that she was sorry she'd left you. Could it have been that, Pat?"

"It could have been. Yes, that's probably what she meant. What else did she tell you?"

"N-nothing. She was very vague. She'd—been drinking, Pat."

"Drinking? That's a new one for her. Was she working?"

"I didn't get that impression. She didn't tell me where she was living, either. Do you know?"

Pat shook his head, staring at the floor. The three of them had grown up in the same block on Vine, though they weren't of an age. Delia had been twenty-three, and Lois was—let's see, she was thirty and the fairly well paid secretary to a vice president of a text publishing firm. When Pat was twenty-two and freshly in uniform, he'd been Lois' hero, who'd been fifteen. At thirty-three, in another kind of uniform, U.S. Army, he'd been Delia's hero, and she'd been nineteen.

At the moment, he was an old man, and nobody's hero.

Lois said, "I guess you need a drink." She rose. "Don't try to think tonight, Pat. It won't be any good."

"I was without her for four months," he said, mostly to himself. "I got through that. I don't know about this. I don't seem to have any feelings at all. It's like I'm dead."

Her back was to him. "I know. That's the way I felt four years ago." She poured a stiff jolt of rye in the bottom of a tumbler.

"Four years ago?" He was only half listening.

"When you married her." She had no expression on her face as she walked over to him. Her hand was steady, holding out the drink.

He looked up to meet her gaze. "Lois, what are you—?"

"I just wanted you to know," she said, "and now. I'm glad you didn't tell that officer you knew me. That's a gesture I can hang on to. It will warm me, this winter."

"Lois—" he protested.

"Drink your drink," she said quietly. "Bottoms up."

He stared at her, and at the glass. He lifted it high and drained it. He could feel its warmth, and then he started to tremble.

"You're one of those black Irishmen," Lois said softly, "who can go all to hell over something like this. And wind up in the gutter. Or examine yourself a little better and decide she was a girl headed for doom from the day of her birth and all you really loved was her beauty."

"Stop talking, Lois. You're all worked up. I'd kill anybody else who talked like that, but I know you loved her, too?"

"Who didn't love her? She was the most beautiful thing alive. But she was a kid, and she'd never be anything else. Even now you can see that, can't you?"

Pat stared at his empty glass, and rose.

"Thanks for the drink," he said, and walked to the door. There he paused, faced her. "It was probably a silly gesture, covering you. There'll be a million people who can tell them who Lois is. I'm sorry I got you up."

"Pat," she said, but he was through the door.

He caught a glimpse of her as he stepped into the elevator. She was like a statue, both hands on the door frame, watching him wordlessly. . . .

The Chief called him in, next morning. He was a big man and a blunt one. He said, "Callender tells me you want a transfer to Homicide for the time being."

Pat nodded, "Yes, sir."

"How is it you didn't tell Callender about this Lois

Weldon last night? A half dozen people have told him about her since."

"I wasn't thinking last night, sir."

The Chief nodded. "You're too close to it, Sergeant. For anybody else, that would be withholding evidence. I'm overlooking it. But I'm denying your request for a temporary transfer to Homicide."

Pat stared at him, saying nothing.

The Chief stared back at him. "You'll want a few days leave."

"Maybe more." He omitted the "sir."

The Chief frowned and looked at his desk top. His eyes came up, again. "I don't like to hammer at you at a time like this. But why *more*? Were you planning to work on this outside of the department?"

Pat nodded.

"If I gave you a direct order not to that would be insubordination, Sergeant."

Pat said nothing.

The Chief said, "Those are my orders."

Pat took out his wallet and unpinned the badge. He laid it on the Chief's desk. "This isn't easy, sir, after fifteen years." He stood up, momentarily realizing what a damn fool speech that had been.

"You're being dramatic," the Chief said evenly. "The thing that makes a good officer is impartiality. Last night you tried to cover a friend. In your present mood, you might go gunning on a half-baked lead and do a lot of damage. This department isn't run that way. But it's your decision, Sergeant." He picked up the badge.

Pat started for the door, and the Chief's voice stopped him. "It would be smart to stay out of Lieutenant Callender's way."

Pat went out without answering. He stood there, in the main hall of Headquarters, feeling like a stranger for the first time in fifteen years. It was then he remembered Lois saying, *You're one of those black Irishmen who can go all to hell.* . . .

He wasn't that complicated, whether she knew it or not. His wife had been killed and it was a personal business with him. His job for fifteen years had been to protect the soft from violence and fraud and chicanery, and this time it was closer to home. Only a fool would expect him to continue checking pawn shops; he hadn't thought the Chief was a fool. But then, it wasn't the Chief's wife.

Detective Prokowski came along the hall and stopped at the sight of Pat.

Pat asked, "What did you find out at Dreamland last night, Steve?"

Prokowski licked his lower lip, frowning.

"Orders, Steve?" Pat asked quietly. "From the lieutenant?"

Prokowski didn't answer that. "Did your transfer go through?"

"No. I've left the force. Don't you want to talk about Dreamland? I won't remind you how long we've known each other."

"Keep your voice down," Prokowski said. "I'll see you at Irv's, at one-thirty."

"Sure. Thanks, Steve."

Irv's wasn't a cops' hangout. Prokowski was a Middle Westerner, originally, and a perfectionist regarding the proper temperature of draught beer. Irv had it at the proper temperature.

It was a hot day, for fall, and the beer was cool enough to sweat the glass without being cold enough to chill the stomach. Pat drank a couple of glasses, waiting for Steve.

Steve came in at a quarter to two and Irv had a glass waiting for him by the time he reached the bar.

He was a big man, Steve Prokowski, and sweating like a college crew man right now. "Nothing," he said wearily. "Lots of guys danced with her. Nothing there. Shoe clerks and CPA's and punk kids. There was a guy they called Helgy. That name mean anything to you, Pat?"

Pat lied with a shake of the head. "This Helgy something special?"

"Danced with her a lot. Took her home. Brought her a couple of times. The way it is, I guess, if you really *like* to dance there's only one place to do it where you've got the room and the right music. That's a place like Dreamland."

"I mean you can't catalogue a guy because he goes to a public dancehall any more than you can catalogue people because you saw them in Grand Central Station. All kinds of people like to dance. This Helgy drove a smooth car, a convertible. That's nightclub stuff, right? But he liked to dance, and the story is, he really could."

Steve finished his beer and Irv brought another. Steve said casually, "Now, what do you know, Pat?"

"I'm out of a job. I don't know anything beyond that. The Chief acted on Callender's recommendation, I suppose?"

"I don't know. The lieutenant doesn't always confide in me. What can you do alone, Pat?"

"It wasn't my idea to work alone." Pat climbed off his stool and put a dollar on the bar. "Out of that, Irv, all of them." He put a hand on Steve's shoulder. "Thanks for coming in."

"You're welcome. Thanks for the beer. I still work for the department, remember, Pat."

"I didn't forget it for a minute."

He could feel Steve's eyes on him in the mirror as he walked out.

Once at breakfast, Delia had been reading the paper and she'd said, "Well, imagine that!"

"I'll try," he'd said. "Imagine what?"

"This boy I used to dance with at Dreamland, this Joe Helgeson. He's a composer, it says here. He likes to dance, and always has, and he knows very little about music, but he's composed. And he must be rich. Helgy, we always called him."

"You should have married him," Pat told her, "so you could have your breakfast in bed."

"There's always time," she told him. "But right now I'm happy with you."

After that, Pat had been conscious of the name. He saw it on sheet music, and it disturbed him. He heard Delia talk to friends about the composer she knew, Helgy, as though that was her world.

He swung his coupe away from the curb and headed toward the Drive. He knew the building, Delia had pointed it out to him once.

It was about eleven stories high with terrace apartments overlooking the bay. Helgy had one of the terrace apartments.

There was a clerk in the quiet lobby, too, and his glance said Pat should have used the service entrance.

Pat said, "Would you phone Mr. Helgeson and tell him Delia Kelley's husband would like very much to talk to him?"

The clerk studied him for a moment before picking up the phone.

He looked surprised when he said, "Mr. Helgeson will see you, sir."

The elevator went up quickly and quietly, and Pat stepped out onto the lush, sculptured carpeting of the top floor. There was a man waiting for him there, a thin man with blond hair in a crew cut, and alert blue eyes.

"Sergeant Kelley?"

Pat nodded.

"I've—been reading the papers. It's—I really don't know what to say, Sergeant."

"I don't either," Pat said, "except to ask you what you might know about it."

. . .

They were walking along the hall, now. They came to the entry hall of the apartment, and Helgeson closed the door behind them. There he faced Pat honestly.

"I've seen her a few times, Sergeant, since she—she left you. There was nothing, well, nothing wrong about it."

"That part doesn't matter," Pat said. "I'm not looking for the men who flirted with her. I'm looking for the man who killed her."

They went into a low, long living room with a beamed ceiling, with floor-length windows facing on the terrace. Helgeson sat in a chair near the huge, bleached mahogany piano.

"I can't help you with that," he said. "I danced with her, at Dreamland. I don't know what attraction the place had for me, except it was the only magic I knew as a kid. I never probed myself for any reasons. She was—a wonderful dancer. I didn't think of her beyond that. That sounds phony, I know, but—" His voice died.

"I'm surprised the Homicide section hasn't sent a man to see you, or have they? You said you'd been reading about it."

"Homicide? No. Why should they?"

"You're pretty well known, and they have your nickname."

"I'm not known down there, not generally. Not as the composer. I'm just another punk, just Helgy, down there. A rather aging punk." He stared at Pat. "But if you know, they know."

Pat shook his head. "I've left the force. I asked to be assigned to this case and was refused."

"Oh," Helgeson rubbed his forehead frowningly. "She told me, when she phoned to break a date yesterday, that she was going back to you. I thought—"

"Yesterday?" Pat interrupted. "She told you *that*, yesterday?"

Helgeson nodded, studying Pat quietly.

Pat could see the pulse in his wrist and he had a passing moment of giddiness. "Where was she living?"

"The Empire Court, over on Hudson."

"Working, was she?"

"I don't think so. She never mentioned it, if she was. She was kind of reticent about all that."

Pat looked at Helgeson levelly. "Was she—living alone?"

Helgeson took a deep breath. "I don't know. I never went in, over there. She was always ready when I called for her." He seemed pale and his voice was unsteady.

Pat felt resentment moving through him, but he couldn't hate them all. Everybody had loved Delia.

He said quietly, "There's nothing you know? She must have mentioned some names, or what she was doing. What the hell did you talk about?"

"We didn't talk much. We danced, that's all. Sergeant, believe me, if I could help I would." His voice was ragged. "If you knew how much I—wanted to help." He shook his head. "There isn't anything I know, not a damned thing."

"All right. I can believe that. If there's anything you

hear or happen to remember, *anything at all*, phone me." He gave him the number.

He went from there to the Empire Court, on Hudson. It was a fairly modern, U-shaped building of gray stone, set back on a deep lot. There was a department car among the cars at the curb.

The name in the lobby read: *Delia Revolt*. Pat pressed the button and the door buzzed.

It was on the second floor and he walked up. There were some technical men dusting for prints, and there was Lieutenant Callender, his back to the doorway, standing in the middle of the living room.

He turned and saw Pat. His face showed nothing.

"Anything?" Pat asked him.

"Look, Pat, for the love of—"

"You look," Pat said. "She was my wife. You got a wife, Lieutenant?"

"I'm married to my second, now." He shook his big head and ran a hand through his hair. "The Chief said you'd resigned."

"That's right "

"You've been a cop for fifteen years. You're acting like a rookie."

"I've only been a husband for four years, Lieutenant. I'm not getting in your way."

"We'll probably get a million prints, all but the right ones. We found a dressing robe we're checking, and some pajamas." The lieutenant's eyes looked away. "I'll talk to the Chief, Pat. I'll see that you get your job back."

"I don't want it back—yet. Thanks, anyway, Lieu-

tenant." He kept seeing Delia in the room and somebody else, some formless, faceless somebody, and the
giddiness came again and he knew he wouldn't have
the stomach to look in any of the other rooms.

He turned his back on the lieutenant and went down
the steps to the lobby and out into the hot, bright day.
They were right about it, of course. A cop shouldn't
be on a family case any more than a surgeon should.
Emotion was no asset in this business.

He sat in the car for minutes, trying to get back to
reality, trying to forget that cozy apartment and the
lieutenant's words. The brightness of the day seemed
to put a sharp outline on things, to give them a sense
of unreality, like a lighted stage setting.

He heard last night's trumpet again, and started the
motor.

The alley was bright, now, but no cleaner. The
voices of the freight handlers on the street side of the
warehouse were drowned by the racket of the huge
trucks bumping past. He walked to the alley's dead end
and saw, for the first time, the door that led from the
dancehall, a fire exit.

It was open, now, and he could see some men in
there, sprinkling the floor with some granulated stuff.
There was the sound of a huge rotary brush polisher,
but it was outside his line of vision.

He went in through the open door, along a wide hall
that flanked the west edge of the bandstand. The men
looked at him curiously as he stood there, imagining
what it must have been like last night. He could almost

hear the music and see the dim lights and the crowded floor.

Along this edge the floor was raised and there were seats up here, for the speculative males, looking over the field, discussing the old favorites and the new finds, wondering what happened to this transient queen and that one. Some had married and not retired.

One of the workers called over, "Looking for the boss, mister?"

"That's right."

"Won't be in this afternoon. The joint's been full of cops and he went out to get some fresh air."

"Okay." Pat turned and went out.

It was nearly five now. He turned the car in a U-turn and headed for Borden. He parked on a lot near Borden and Sixth, and walked the two blocks to Curtes-Husted, Publishers.

Lois was busily typing when he opened the door to the outer office. She looked up at his entrance, and her face seemed to come alive, suddenly.

"Pat!" She got up and came over to the railing.

"I was pretty rough, last night. I thought a drink and dinner might take us back to where we were. Part way, anyway."

"It will, it will Oh, Pat, if you knew what last night—" She put a hand on his on top of the railing.

The door to Pat's right opened, and a man stood there. He had a masculine, virile face and iron-gray hair. He said, "You can go any time, Lois. I guess Mr. Curtes won't be back."

"Thank you, Mr. Husted,' she said. "I'll be going in a minute."

He smiled, and closed the door.

"My boss, the VP," she whispered. "Isn't he handsome?"

"I suppose." Pat could feel her hand trembling.

She said quietly, "You're better, aren't you? You're coming out of it."

"I'm better," he said. "This whole case is one blind alley."

"Delia knew a lot of men—of people I'll be with you in a minute."

They went to the *Lamp Post*, an unpretentious restaurant nearby.

They had a martini each, and Lois told him, "Their spare ribs are the best in town."

He ordered the spare ribs.

She seemed animated. She said, "It's going to be all right. It's going to take some time, and then you're going to be really happy, Pat. I'm going to see that you're happy."

He ordered another pair of drinks, and they finished those before the ribs came. They went from the *Lamp Post* to a spot on the west side, and Pat tried very hard to get drunk. But it didn't work; the alcohol didn't touch him.

They went back to Lois' place. He sat with her in the car in front of her apartment.

"Come on up," she said. "I'll make some coffee."

He shook his head. "I know Husted was paying for

that apartment Delia was living in. I've known it for two months, Lois. And you did, too, didn't you?"

Her silence was his answer.

"You probably thought Husted killed her, and yet you've told the police nothing. Delia probably told you yesterday or the day before that she was coming back to me. But you didn't tell me that. Was it yesterday you saw her?"

"The day before. I didn't want her to come back, Pat. And I didn't tell you about my boss because he's got a family, because he's a fundamentally decent man."

"You didn't want her to come back. Because of me?" Pat's voice was hoarse. "You poor damned fool, you don't know me, do you? No matter what she was, Lois, I'll be married to her the rest of my life. But you were the one who could have told me she was coming back. You could have saved her life."

"Pat—"

"Get out, Lois. Get out—quick!"

She scrambled out.

The liquor was getting to him a little now. He finished the note, there on his dinette table, and then went to unlock the front door. Then he called headquarters, gave them the message, and went to pick up the note. He read:

Lieutenant Callender:

I wanted to work with Homicide because I thought it would be safer that way. I could see how close you boys were getting. But it doesn't matter now, because I've no desire to escape you. I killed my wife with a wrecking bar which you'll find in the luggage deck of my car. I couldn't stand the thought of her loving anyone else and I wasn't man enough to rid myself of her. The checking I've done today reveals to me I would probably have escaped detection. I make this confession of my own free will.

Sergeant Patrick Kelley

He waited then, .38 in hand. He waited until he heard the wail of the siren, and a little longer. He waited until he heard the tires screeching outside.

Then he put the muzzle of his .38 to the soft roof of his mouth, and pulled the trigger

Subscription to THE NEW BLACK MASK QUARTERLY

$27.80/year in the U.S.

Subscription correspondence should be sent to

THE NEW BLACK MASK QUARTERLY

129 West 56th Street

New York, NY 10019

U.S.A.